Evan's kiss was everything she remembered and more.

Unhurried but hungry, it promised all kinds of pleasures to come, and pure *want* drowned out any caution from her higher brain functions.

He tasted like the whiskey on the rocks he'd been drinking earlier—only hot and far more potent. Then he leaned into her, pressing her back against the cool cinderblock wall, deepening the kiss and blocking out everything that wasn't him.

And his hands… One was gentle against her cheek, but the other was strong against her hip—and both of them were caressing her, stoking the fire kindled by his tongue.

She slid her hands under his jacket to feel the hard muscles of his stomach hidden under fine cotton, then wrapped her arms around his waist to pull him against her.

A groan echoed off the walls and she wasn't sure if it was hers or his. Evan's lips were hot against her neck, sending shivers over her skin.

Dear Reader

You may remember from my bio that I used to dance. Not at Olivia's level, of course, but writing this book was, in many ways, a trip down memory lane—taking me back to some of the best (not to mention thinnest and most flexible) days of my life. Ballet was always my first love, and the first dream I chased, and it was so much fun to revisit that world. Thanks for indulging me in this!

Had I ended up with Olivia's career, I like to think there would have been an Evan in *my* story, too. (Hey, if I'm going to dream I might as well dream big!) Evan…*sigh*. So cocky and sure, yet still haunted by his own insecurities. Plus, he's hot and not threatened by Olivia's success. Yeah, I fell in love with him pretty easily.

I hope you come to love Evan and Olivia as much as I do. As always, I'd love to hear from you, either through my website, www.BooksByKimberly.com, or on Facebook or Twitter.

All the best

Kimberly

THE MILLION-DOLLAR QUESTION

BY
KIMBERLY LANG

Published in Great Britain 2014
by Mills & Boon, an imprint of Harlequin (UK) Limited,
Eton House, 18-24 Paradise Road, Richmond, Surrey, TW9 1SR

© 2014 Kimberly Kerr

ISBN: 978-0-263-91155-8

Harlequin (UK) Limited's policy is to use papers that are natural,
renewable and recyclable products and made from wood grown in
sustainable forests. The logging and manufacturing processes conform
to the legal environmental regulations of the country of origin.

Printed and bound in Spain
by Blackprint CPI, Barcelona

Kimberly Lang hid romance novels behind her textbooks in junior high, and even a Master's programme in English couldn't break her obsession with dashing heroes and happily-ever-after. A ballet dancer turned English teacher, Kimberly married an electrical engineer and turned her life into an ongoing episode of *When Dilbert Met Frasier*. She and her Darling Geek live in beautiful North Alabama, with their one Amazing Child—who, unfortunately, shows an aptitude for sports.

Visit Kimberly at www.booksbykimberly.com for the latest news—and don't forget to say hi while you're there!

Other Modern Tempted™ titles by Kimberly Lang:

NO TIME LIKE MARDI GRAS
LAST GROOM STANDING

**This and other titles by Kimberly Lang
are available in eBook format
from www.millsandboon.co.uk**

DEDICATION

To Marilynn, Terri, Sunny, Angela, Stacey, Marbury,
both Melissas, Anna, Andrea, India, Kelly, Buddy, Chris,
Susan, Nelson and the whole ASFA dance department
for all the stories that start with,
"There was this one time, during *Nutcracker*…"

CHAPTER ONE

"Somebody's got a hot date."

It was hard for Olivia Madison to both roll her eyes and apply mascara at the same time, but she managed it—just barely. Rehearsals had run long today and she was now running late. She didn't have time for this. "It's not a date."

Her roommate, Annie, flopped across the bed and examined the outfit Olivia had laid out for tonight. "Hmm…Silky top, the 'good butt' jeans and 'take me' boots. You curled your hair, you're wearing makeup, and…" She stopped to sniff the air delicately. "I smell perfume. All signs point to a hot date. And it's about time. I was getting afraid we'd have to get a couple of cats soon and the lease doesn't allow pets."

"First of all, neither of us is in Cat Lady territory just yet. Getting married and having babies is what your thirties are for. Second, it's just dinner. Pretty much a business dinner, at that."

Annie still wasn't convinced. "In that outfit? Please. Did you shave your legs?"

Olivia had, but that was neither here nor there and had nothing to do with the person she was meeting for dinner. "It's with my brother's college roommate, for goodness sake."

"Is he cute?"

Olivia had to admit he was. She'd looked him up online to see if he'd changed much in the past nine years, rather hoping to find that he'd developed a paunch or lost a lot of hair, only to be disappointed in that hope. If anything, the past decade had been quite good to Evan Lawford, maturing his features—and even the attitude he projected in the photos—light-years past the frat rat she remembered. The sun-bleached hair had turned darker, probably meaning he didn't spend as much time on the beach as he used to, but the color offset his blue eyes nicely. The cheekbones and the jawline she remembered quite well, only the two-day stubble look was also gone. The difference between boy and man was stark and startling at first.

Objectively speaking, Evan Lawford was *hot*. Male-model-broodingly-advertising-expensive-suits-in-a-glossy-magazine hot. "It doesn't really matter. He's a jerk."

"Which means he *is* a hottie, and that's just wrong." Annie sighed and rolled to her back. "Why can't the really nice guys be drop-dead gorgeous, too? Is that really too much to ask?" she pleaded to the universe.

"All signs point to *yes*." Olivia tossed the mascara tube back into her makeup bag. *Jerk* was a nice word for Evan. He was a cocky, arrogant, ego-ridden player.

But he was a *successful* cocky, arrogant, ego-ridden player, and that was what was important at the moment. She'd have to suck it up and deal with the rest.

"So why are you having dinner with him then?"

Because I'm forced to sell myself out in order to further my career. That wasn't entirely exactly true: no one at the Miami Modern Ballet Company expected her to actually sleep with someone for their money, but the trade-off still gave her icky vibes. "I need him to sponsor me."

Annie's forehead wrinkled in concern. "Like a twelve-step kind of sponsor? Are you okay?"

Olivia kept the sigh—and the smart-ass comeback—behind her teeth. It wasn't all that unexpected of a speculation, and at least Annie was asking it from a place of concern. Olivia had left home at fifteen to spend the next decade in studios and on stages, driving herself to reach this point: a contracted principal in an established, prestigious ballet company. Therefore, everyone assumed that she had to have something wrong with her—drug habit, an eating disorder, or even just a flat-out psychotic break à la *Black Swan* picked up along the way. She nearly snorted. There probably *was* something wrong with her, only they didn't have an official diagnosis for it yet.

And while she'd known Annie for only a few months—trading the privacy of having her own place for the opportunity to live near the beaches and nightlife of Miami, even with an unknown roommate—they were getting along very well. "Not that kind of sponsor. An actual please-donate-your-money kind of sponsor."

Annie looked confused. "You're fundraising?"

"In a way. Money is tight all over, and the arts are really feeling the pinch," she explained, slipping into her jeans. Annie averted her eyes as Olivia dressed, but Olivia had lost any kind of modesty years ago through one too many quick changes backstage in view of the entire corps and stagehands. "Our state funding has been slashed, ticket sales are down and corporate sponsorship in general is not as strong as it used to be. So nowadays, rich people can adopt a dancer of their very own. In return, they get all kinds of perks—tickets, backstage passes, first dibs on tables at the En Pointe Ball and for the big spenders," Olivia continued, as she pasted a smile on her face and added a chipper tone, "the chance to have their dancer appear at their corporate—or sometimes private—events."

"That sounds cool." Her forehead wrinkled. "But kinda creepy, too."

"Tell me about it."

"And you need one of these sponsors? I thought you had a contract."

Annie, who worked as a Spanish-language interpreter for the city, was getting a crash course in the state of the arts in America these days. "I do, but my contract isn't cheap. And while MMBC has the option to pick up my contract for next season, there's no guarantee that they will—especially if I'm the only one without sponsorship to offset my cost. Sponsorship doesn't guarantee anything either way, but it won't hurt."

"I see. So you're hoping your brother's college room-mate has that kind of money?"

"I know he does. I haven't seen Evan in years, but he and Jory are still real tight." Why that was, she didn't quite know. Evan had nearly succeeded in turn-ing Jory into a carbon copy of himself in college, and while Jory had turned out okay anyway, she didn't re-ally understand what the two men could possibly have in common. "He's got the money." She frowned at the mirror as she finger-combed out the curls and sprayed her hair into place. "I just need to figure out how to ask him for it."

"Why can't you just ask him outright? It seems pretty straightforward, and it's a tax deduction to boot."

"Yeah, but it's…" She wasn't sure how to explain it, even if she wanted to. Which she really didn't. "It's complicated."

"Complicated?" Annie's forehead wrinkled again, then smoothed out as understanding dawned. "*Oh. That* kind of complicated."

"Let's just say that it's not complicated enough to keep me from asking, but complicated enough to make me want to handle the situation delicately."

"If it's going to be awkward, why not just call your brother instead? Get him to play middleman."

"No." *No way.* That was a can of worms she defi-nitely wasn't going to open.

"Then maybe your brother or your parents could sponsor you, instead?"

She knew Jory. Telling him she needed sponsorship—or any money, really—would lead him to opening his checkbook. He'd tell Mom and Daddy, and they'd want to do the same. And that was *not* going to happen. Jory needed to be investing his money into his own business, and Mom and Daddy needed to be saving for retirement.

Mom and Daddy were comfortable enough, but they'd sacrificed greatly over the years to support her dream. So had Jory, in fact. She wasn't going to take another blessed dime from them. Any of them.

She shook her head. "They're in Tampa, and the sponsors need to be local." Even as she said it, she had no idea if it was true. The company probably assumed sponsors would be local—and that was how the donor rewards were structured—but she couldn't imagine any company turning down money, regardless of the source. Still, it was a clean and quick explanation, and Annie accepted it at face value.

"That's a problem, then."

"And I've been in Miami for only three months. I don't really know anyone else." She paused in zipping up her boots to look hopefully at Annie. "Unless you happen to have thousands of dollars tucked away and a hidden, burning desire to support the arts in your community?"

Annie shook her head. "Uh, no."

"Then I'm off to dinner with Evan." She took one

last critical look in the mirror, then turned to Annie. "How do I look?"

"Amazing, as always. And, as always, I kinda hate you for it. If you can't win Evan over with logic or reason, you should be able to flirt his checkbook right open." Annie rolled off the bed and got to her feet. With a cheeky grin, she added, "I won't wait up for you."

Olivia had no intention of flirting with Evan at all. She could be polite and friendly, but this was merely business. She'd flirted with him that one time, and the lessons learned stuck with her to this day. But she was older now, wiser, and she could look back on it for the educational experience it was, without feeling the pain or shame.

Much.

The restaurant Evan chose to meet her at was only about six blocks from the condo she shared with Annie, and Olivia elected to walk it. Eventually, she'd have to buy a car—an expense she'd managed to avoid for at least the past five years—but for now, Miami's public transport could get her pretty much anywhere her feet couldn't.

It might be November, but she didn't need a sweater. However, she grabbed a pashmina in case the air conditioning in the restaurant was set on "Arctic." After spending so many winters in more northern climes, it was so *so* nice to be back in Florida, with her winter gear shipped home to Tampa to the storage unit she kept there. The sun had been down for an hour, but the temperatures were still in the high seventies, perfect for a walk, but it was a little jarring for it to be that warm as businesses took down their Halloween decorations and replaced them with a mix of turkeys and Santa Claus.

She could come to really love Miami. MMBC was a highly respected company with a great mix of classical and contemporary in their repertoire. It may be not as prestigious as some in New York, but the trade-off was a lower cost of living and fewer up-and-comers nipping at her heels all the time. She could still do the occasional guest artist thing when the traveling bug bit her or things started to feel stale, but Miami was a great base.

And she needed to start thinking about the future, anyway. If all went well, she could get another six, maybe seven, years in before retiring, but she was feeling the effects of the past two decades already and her chances of injury increased each year. She needed to be building some kind of foundation, and Miami was ideal for that.

Plus, it was only four hours from home.

All this was great. Provided she could keep the job she'd worked so hard to get. The fact she was willing to turn to Evan Lawford proved how much she wanted her contract picked up for next season. That would give her time to build a reputation and network here in Miami and increase her chances of further seasons exponentially.

She just had to get through dinner with Evan and get his agreement first.

Easy-peasy, right?

Oddly, Evan hadn't asked many questions when she'd emailed him, saying hello and asking if he'd like to get together. She'd provided her phone number, but he'd stuck to email, setting up the place and time with the minimum amount of communication necessary. She wasn't sure if that was a good thing or a not.

It had taken courage—more than she thought she'd need for something so simple—to email him in the first place, but he'd accepted so quickly that she'd only had forty-eight hours to figure out how to actually pull this off.

Evan and Jory were friends, practically brothers. Although she'd not been there to see it, she knew Evan loved her parents and had spent a lot of weekends and holidays at their house instead of his own. Her parents loved him. But that had nothing to do with her, and she couldn't cash in on her parents' kindness or Jory's friendship like some kind of promissory note owed to her.

But *they* weren't friends. They were just two people in Jory's orbit, basically little more than strangers.

Okay, they were *more* than strangers. She just wasn't sure where on the hierarchy of relationships to place her brother's roommate when he was also the guy you lost your virginity to in what turned out to be only slightly more than a one-night stand.

Ugh.

While she'd felt hurt and used at the time, perspective could offer the balm that it probably hadn't been personal. And realistically, he'd most likely saved her from making a similar mistake later on—when she would have been alone, surrounded by strangers, and even more vulnerable. Naïveté was a dangerous thing.

The truly embarrassing part was that she'd known exactly what he was going in to it. Hell, he'd taken Jory into his decadent world of wine, women and song, debauching him quite thoroughly. But with the arrogance only a teenager could have, she'd believed she was different. *Special.*

Combined with Evan's combo of charm, good looks and raw sensuality, that arrogance had easily overwhelmed and shouted down anything she'd known merely intellectually.

That was the rational, reasonable part of her brain. The same part of her brain that turned that burn into something useful, allowing her to focus on her training instead of getting wrapped up in messy entanglements that could have complicated her life unnecessarily. So that was good.

Parties, boyfriends…all those things she'd been told she'd have to sacrifice for her career didn't seem like so much of a sacrifice after that. Or at least not an overly painful one.

Her inner eighteen-year-old still held a grudge about it, but she'd need to keep *that* safely hidden away.

Even if *Evan* felt remorse over the whole sorry incident, she wasn't sure that was something she could— or wanted to—play on, either. She'd look foolish and ridiculous and hopelessly naive—and petty and manipulative to boot.

Nope. That little lost weekend needed to stay lost.

She was an adult; he was an adult. This was a purely business transaction, albeit with a personal glaze. But there was no crime in networking the contacts you had, personal or not.

Be friendly. Be businesslike. Evan was a successful businessman. According to Jory, Evan's advertising agency was growing in phenomenal leaps and bounds, and he should appreciate a professional approach. There was no need to jump right in with the request—a little pleasant small talk always greased the wheels nicely. She would put the sponsorship out on the table early, giving him plenty of time for questions and plenty of time for her to convince him. If all went well, she could walk out of here tonight with his commitment and the ballet's business manager could get the good news by class tomorrow.

If all went well.

And there was no reason why it shouldn't.

"Good evening, Mr. Lawford."

The valet at Tourmaine opened Evan's door and greeted him with a smile. Tourmaine was his go-to place for entertaining clients—modern enough to feel on trend without being trendy, music loud enough to hear and enjoy without hindering conversations, and, most importantly, good food and a staff that knew him—and his tipping habits—well. "Good evening, Brian."

"Enjoy your meal."

"Thank you." A banal, basic exchange of pleasantries, but one that he needed to remind him that the world hadn't, in fact, gone insane.

Because barring that, he had no idea why Olivia Madison wanted to have dinner with him.

He knew, of course, that she'd moved to Miami. Jory had been ridiculously proud of his sister's accomplishment, and they'd had dinner back in the fall when Jory came to see Olivia's first performance with her new company. But Olivia hadn't joined them, and Jory didn't bring up his sister unnecessarily.

Evan hadn't seen Olivia since she was eighteen, and that was definitely intentional. The only thing that had ever come between him and Jory was Olivia, and they'd nearly come to blows over her, doing damage to their friendship that had taken time to repair. He didn't know how twitchy Jory might be about it these days, but it wasn't something he wanted to stir up—not until he at least knew why Olivia had contacted him in the first place.

Miami was plenty big enough for them to never come in contact with each other at all, and he assumed that was exactly how Olivia—and Jory, as well—wanted it.

So an email out of the blue from her with a dinner invitation had to be viewed with some level of suspicion, yet there was no way he could not have come. If only to find out why.

Yep, that was his story and he was sticking to it.

He was a few minutes early, but Olivia was already there, the unusual coppery-blond hair both Madison siblings inherited from their mother easy to spot in the small crowd of people around the bar. She was in profile to him, reading something on her phone, giving him the chance to examine her at leisure.

She'd been baby-faced at eighteen, but far more mature in some ways than others her age—by then, she'd already traveled and lived abroad, a professional in her career when most others were still figuring out their future. She'd said she'd wanted a taste of real college life, the same as anyone else, and there hadn't been a good reason not to indulge her—and himself at the same time.

The baby face was now gone, replaced by chiseled cheekbones and winged eyebrows that gave her a classical, elegant look, emphasized by the impossibly good posture and movements that were effortlessly graceful—even those as simple as ordering a drink or walking toward him…which she was now doing, a hesitant smile on her face.

"Evan. It's good to see you."

While her tone sounded sincere, he doubted it was completely true. There was a moment of hesitation, then she leaned in for one of those air-kiss things. Her cheek touched his accidentally and she jumped back as if she'd been scalded. He wouldn't deny it: it sent a bit of a jolt through him, as well. He cleared his throat. "And you."

The initial pleasantries finished, they stood there in an awkward silence, and he wasn't used to awkward silences. "You look good," he managed.

There was a small tug of her lips that stopped short of a smile. "So do you."

More silence.

Thankfully, the hostess arrived to save them. "Mr. Lawford, we have your table ready."

Following Olivia to the table gave him another chance to study her, and goodness, she was thin. She'd always been on the slight side, a necessity of dancing, but *wraithlike* was the word that came to mind. It was a good thing they were in a restaurant, because the need to feed her something was nearly overwhelming. She was also taller than he remembered, just a couple of inches shorter than his six-two, and only part of that height came from the boots she was wearing.

Long soft curls hung to the middle of her back, and a gold chain belt hung loosely around her tiny waist. Mile-long legs ended at slightly turned-out feet, giving her walk an unusual cadence that was still somehow graceful and smooth. Chin up and shoulders back, Olivia had presence.

He couldn't take his eyes off her. And that had gotten him in trouble before.

He shook his head to clear it. *Of course* the woman was thin and graceful. She *had* to be. That was a job requirement, and from what little he did know, Olivia Madison was good at her job.

Safely seated in the high-walled booth he favored

for its privacy, the awkward silence that had started in the bar was easy to fill with menu discussions and ordering. He couldn't stop his eyes from widening as she ordered a meal almost as big as his, and as the server walked away, she noticed. "What?"

"That's a lot of food."

She shot him a look. "If it's a problem, I'm perfectly happy to pay for my own dinner."

"That's not what I meant."

An eyebrow arched up. "Really? What did you mean then?"

Her tone could be called innocent and inquiring, but he realized the danger underneath just a second too late to pull the words back. "It's…well, you…" He usually wasn't foolish enough to bring up weight and diet with any woman, but he'd already stepped into it. "I guess I expected you to order a small salad with dressing on the side."

She snorted. "Maybe for the *first* course. But I spent six hours in rehearsals today. I'm hungry."

"Okay, a *large* salad, then," he teased.

Olivia folded her hands primly on the table, and as she spoke, her tone clearly said this was a speech she'd given many times before. "I eat. I have to. I work my body hard, and my body needs fuel to do that work. I stay aware of my weight, but not in an unhealthy manner. Since I'm not obsessing over it, I'd appreciate it if you didn't either. Okay?"

Duly chastised, he nodded. "Okay."

Then she leaned forward. "And seriously, they put

blue cheese *cream* sauce on a *steak* here. How am I *not* going to order that?"

"Fair enough." She talked a good game, but he'd withhold judgment until he actually saw her eat something. He worked in advertising, for goodness sake. He knew about models and the things they did to lose weight, but he had to admit that Olivia wasn't skeletal or starving—she was very slim, yes, but she didn't have the hollowed-out sickly look. "It's just surprising."

She inclined her head, and reached for her water.

"But not as surprising as hearing from you."

Olivia's hand froze, making him suspicious all over again. She recovered quickly, though. "I'm just full of surprises then. Honestly, I feel I've been rather rude not getting in touch before now. My only excuse is that I've been unbelievably busy the last few weeks—getting settled, with rehearsals for the fall performance, and then straight into *The Nutcracker* and the winter special that's coming up in January…I haven't had time to even think."

He'd known Jory for over twelve years, and his sister shared many of his mannerisms, making her somewhat easier to read than the average person. Olivia wasn't fully at ease in this conversation, which wasn't surprising. There were many reasons—beyond the busyness of her life—not to have been in touch before now, but there was no sense bringing those up just yet. That piqued his curiosity further, but he found that he wanted to make her comfortable, nonetheless. The past was bound to come up eventually, and it would be better to have a friendly footing before that happened. "But you're feeling more settled in now?"

"Yeah. I'm not getting hopelessly lost every time I leave the house these days, which is good. And it's nice to be home in Florida, where I can go to the beach anytime I want. Even in November."

Via Jory, he knew Olivia had done recent stays in Chicago and Boston, where the snow would be enough to drive any Florida native to the brink of insanity. "Which beach is your favorite?"

Her mouth twisted. "I haven't actually gone, yet. Like I said, I've been busy."

"Are you some kind of workaholic?"

"I believe that when you love your job, it's not exactly drudgery to put the time in."

"That's not an answer."

"I work a lot, and I like it. How's that?"

"That's a good answer. I might have to use that myself in the future." He paused as the server brought their drinks. Then he lifted his glass to her. "And congratulations on landing the new job."

She accepted his toast, a real smile replacing the hesitant one. "Thanks. It's exciting. MMBC—the company—normally chooses its principals from inside, but they decided to open the search this time. I knew one of the company members from years ago when I first went to New York, and he brought my name up to the artistic director. All the stars just aligned perfectly to get me here." She seemed as if she was just winding up, but caught herself instead, reaching for her wineglass and sitting back against the leather seat. "But what about you? Jory says your agency's doing really well."

"I can't complain. We're only three years old, and we still have some growing to do, but we're good."

"That's great to hear. I'm happy for you." Olivia stared at her glass, pondering the depths of pinot gris, and silence settled again. Then she looked up at him again with that smile he was beginning to think was definitely fake. "Jory's coming down with my parents in a couple of weeks to see the performance."

"I know. We're planning to get together while he's here."

"Oh, good."

"He says your parents are very excited."

"They don't get to see me in action very often because I'm usually so far away. I send videos and stuff, but it's not the same for them. And honestly, I'm excited they're getting to come, too. You know," she added casually, "if you'd like to come with them to the show, I can get you a ticket."

"Oh, hell, no." The words slipped out before he could check them. *Damn it. Insult the woman's career. That's always a great dinner conversation topic.* "I mean, no thank you. I'm not really a fan."

"Of *The Nutcracker* or ballet in general?"

"Both. No offense," he added. "It's just not my thing."

"None taken. We like what we like." She was being gracious, but he still felt as though he'd offended her. "Are you into the arts at all?"

He shrugged. "I used to have a membership to the art museum. I like the Egyptian stuff. There are a few local bands I keep up with." Lord, he sounded like a cultural wasteland. He justified it by saying, "Getting the agency off the ground has kept me pretty busy."

"I'm not judging."

Her smirk implied otherwise. "Yes, you are."

She shrugged a shoulder. "Okay, maybe a little. The arts celebrate what makes us human. They are the cornerstone of civilization and the heart of a community."

He nearly laughed, but swallowed it at the last second. Olivia obviously believed what she was saying. "You should work in advertising. That sounds like copy straight from a fundraising brochure."

She inclined her head. "That doesn't make it less true."

"That doesn't make them less boring, either."

Her eyes widened. "No offense intended again?" she asked.

"Of course."

"You could still support them financially, you know."

He shook his head. "Don't look at me like that."

"Like what?" she asked innocently.

"Like I'm some kind of miser. I give to charity. I just lean toward the more practical. You know, like food, housing, medical care…"

"Those are all very worthy causes."

"Is that sarcasm?"

"No. It's hard to enrich the mind and soul when the

body is hungry. I'm sure your philanthropy is much appreciated."

Evan felt as if there was something else that needed to be addressed. An undercurrent he was missing. But they were interrupted by the arrival of their meals.

Olivia greeted the food with a genuine, "That looks amazing." She inhaled the aroma with a blissful look on her face before taking a bite.

The steak with cream sauce was one of Tourmaine's signature dishes, and rightly so. Olivia obviously agreed; chewing her first bite with her eyes closed while making little happy noises. "Oh, man. That's *so* good."

He swallowed hard. He knew that look. Remembered it as if he'd seen it yesterday. But Olivia hadn't been eating steak with cream sauce the last time he'd seen it. *He'd* put that look on her face.

His blood rushed to his lap with a speed that left him feeling slightly light-headed. That one look had opened a floodgate of memories—memories he'd safely locked in a box to forget until just now. But that look...

He could practically feel those long, strong legs wrapped around him.

When she opened her eyes and saw him staring, she looked a little abashed. "I said I eat. I can't eat like this *all* the time, though, so I enjoy it very much when I do."

If she was going to enjoy her entire dinner like that, he'd be dead by dessert.

Thank goodness Olivia couldn't read his mind.

CHAPTER TWO

EVAN FOUND THAT concentrating on his food helped. Some. Tourmaine's owner, Harry, came by, nicely distracting his attention as he introduced Olivia and she complimented everything from the steak to the music. Harry was duly flattered and invited her back to try everything on the menu.

By the time it was just the two of them again, Evan had himself basically back under control, thankfully.

They ate for a little while, the conversation carefully kept to the simple topics of the excellent food, Jory's successes, her parents and the weather. It was oddly easy. Even fun, at times. There was the occasional over-long pause, but they didn't last. He'd nearly forgotten how smart and funny Olivia could be, and that had only improved in the intervening years. They had very little in common—no overlapping tastes in music, TV or movies, and some widely differing stances on politics and social issues—but that worked in their favor, keeping the conversation moving and interesting. And while he might be shallow, *this* was what had actually tipped the attraction all those years ago and made him risk Jory's wrath.

And it was almost enough to let him ignore that little voice nagging him now.

Almost.

When he decided they'd had enough of the small talk, he charged ahead. "Well, you seem to be settling in fine, so you don't need anything from me in that area, everything is okay with the people we have in common, and," he couldn't help but say through a chuckle, "I don't want to buy season tickets to the ballet. Care to tell me why we're actually here?"

She chewed, but he figured that was more of a stalling tactic than anything else. Finally she swallowed. "To eat dinner?"

"Come on, Liv, you've been in town since when? August? If you'd wanted my company for dinner, you'd have called long before now."

"Therefore, I must have nefarious reasons to do so now?"

"I wouldn't necessarily assume your reasons are nefarious, but you must have at least *one* above and beyond a free meal."

She shrugged a shoulder again.

Fine. There'd been two elephants in the room and Olivia had been talking around them both for over an hour now. If she wouldn't address the specific *why* of this dinner, he'd simply address the problem he did know. He leveled a look at her across the table. "After all, the last time we spoke, you called me a cold, heartless bastard."

She blinked, somehow caught off guard by the blunt statement. "True. I was mad and my feelings were hurt."

At least she was honest about that much. "So why would you want to have dinner with a 'heartless bastard'?"

"I'm trying to make my home here. I thought it'd be nice to expand my network of people outside just the dance world, and you are the only person in Miami—outside my roommate and the company members—that I know. Since I'm not the same person I was nine years ago, I'm assuming you aren't either." The corner of her mouth twitched. "I guess I'm hoping you outgrew that."

"Not really," he said, causing her to choke slightly on her wine.

"Wow." She cleared her throat and thought for a minute. "Well, at least you're honest about it."

"Those aren't exactly bad qualities to have in my line of work."

She thought for a moment, and then nodded. "If that's the case, then we just won't do this again. It's okay. You're friends with Jory and that doesn't automatically include me simply by extension. You have a life, and I can't just intrude upon that."

Well, now he felt like a heel. And the one possibility he'd been steadfastly ignoring as implausible was beginning to win out: Olivia had *wanted* to see him. He'd hurt her and yet she'd still gotten in touch after all this time. It was equal parts flattering and mystifying.

It was also extremely complicated. Jory had put his sister firmly off-limits nine years ago. Not that Evan blamed him. He'd been seriously messed up back then, not nearly good enough for Olivia. Hell, he probably still wasn't what someone like Liv needed, and he had to assume that prohibition was still in place. Of course, Olivia didn't know about any of that. It put him in a very awkward situation. There was a huge difference between an eighteen-year-old and a twenty-seven-year-old, but she was still Jory's sister.

Maybe she was just lonely and in need of a friend. Just because *he* was having flashbacks to happier, more naked times, there was no reason to assume she was, as well. And while he'd broken a major tenet of the Guy Code by sleeping with her before, there was an equally important tenet of the Code that required him to look after a friend's sister when she was new and alone in a big city. There were as many possibilities as pitfalls here. "Well, I guess if you're fully aware I'm *still* a heartless bastard and are willing to accept that, then there's no reason we can't be friends anyway."

Olivia's eyes widened at the baldness of his words, but he could rest easy either way knowing she was coming in with her eyes wide open. The ball was in her court, and he was frankly very curious to find out how she'd play.

Because she couldn't say he hadn't warned her.

You're a coward. A fool. A screaming idiot who should be kept on a leash for her own safety.

Olivia stared at herself in the mirror of the ladies' room and frowned. She'd had such clear, simple goals for this dinner, and she'd failed to accomplish even one.

Instead, she couldn't have made a bigger mess if she'd tried.

In a just and fair world, anger and hurt feelings would not fade enough over time to allow the person who caused those feelings to have the same effect on her that had gotten her into the situation in the first place. Instead of being hit with all the things about Evan she'd hated him for, she'd been overwhelmed with all the things that had sucked her into Evan's bed in the first place.

It was easy enough to say he was charming and good-looking, but it was another to face that head-on. The way that baritone slithered through her insides, turning them to jelly; the way those blue, blue eyes could make the most casual glance feel like a caress. It was even more devastating because he wasn't *trying* to seduce her. That was just his default setting, a natural part of his personality that made him catnip to women.

It was humiliating. She might not have Evan's legions of former lovers, but she wasn't an innocent anymore either. She'd taken lovers, had flings and summer romances, so why was Evan able to reduce her to a simpering virgin again?

Mercy.

She'd been rattled and ready to run for the door the minute she'd laid eyes on him. She should have known then that the whole idea was insane, made her excuses and left instead. But *no*, she just had to try.

Wandering up to a random stranger on the street and asking if they wanted to support the MMBC and adopt a dancer might have been less nerve-racking and equally as successful. And she'd probably like herself a bit more afterward than she did right now.

It hadn't been a completely crazy idea, just one that worked much better in theory than in practice. Regardless of how sensible it sounded on the surface, she hadn't been able to shake that uneasy feeling that swirled underneath, and she was now very glad she hadn't followed, though.

Maybe I'm not a coward. She was a decent human being who'd got carried away for a minute, but pulled back in time. Points for that. And she'd made it through dinner without making a complete fool of herself, so bonus points could be awarded, as well.

Thank goodness Evan could be so blunt, or else she might have tried to pull off this stunt—which she was now viewing as pretty gauche and tacky. She was now going to say good-night and go home, thanking her lucky stars she wasn't leaving in shame.

She'd sort out the other confusing stuff later. Much later, and when she was alone. She took a deep breath and squared her shoulders. *Time for a dignified end to this farce of an evening.*

Evan was waiting for her out front. "Thank you for dinner," she said. "It was good to see you." *Handshake? Air kiss?*

"And you. Do you have your valet ticket?"

"I walked."

"I'll drive you home, then."

"It's only six blocks," she protested, but it sounded weak even to her own ears.

"It's about to rain." As if to punctuate his words, a raindrop landed on her shoulder. *So much for dry Miami Novembers.* It felt like revenge for her tackiness.

Was it worth a standoff? Probably not, and she'd look foolish wanting to walk home in the rain. She was just feeling ashamed of herself in general and didn't want to drag this out any further. Of course, they *could* stand here and continue to argue, but the ridiculousness of that would only exacerbate her foolishness. "Okay. Thanks."

The timing bordered on eerie, as the moment the words left her lips, a car coasted to a stop at the curb and Evan was reaching for the door. The man had to be half genie.

This car was a far cry from the beat-up, perfect-for-trips-to-the-beach Jeep he'd driven in college. Black, low-slung and convertible, it looked expensive and classy, and it suited this adult Evan perfectly.

She wasn't surprised that the valet knew Evan's name—she'd gotten the feeling at dinner that he was a regular here—but the fact Evan knew the valet's name did surprise her. Her experience with rich donors had proved that most of them couldn't be bothered with the little people. He couldn't be *entirely* selfish if he remembered the names of valets and servers.

His car proved that Evan *definitely* had money— regardless of his modest "we're still growing" comments and it was almost enough to make her rethink her original, now aborted, plan.

No. Now she had her mother's voice in her head, reminding her that anything she thought might be a tacky or bad idea probably *was*, and she bit her tongue as Evan put the car in gear.

"Which way?"

"Left at the light," she answered absently. The traffic was bad and the streets were crowded, slowing their progress to a crawl. She definitely could have walked home faster than this. Her original refusal seemed less foolish now, as she was trapped in a small, enclosed space with Evan, his hand only inches from her thigh as he shifted gears.

It created an intimacy she wasn't quite prepared to face at the moment, and in the small space, the silence rapidly gained weight.

When Evan sighed, she knew he felt it, too. "Liv…"

No one but Evan had ever called her Liv. Jory called her Livvy sometimes, but Liv sounded more grown-up and more intimate, somehow. And all things considered, "Liv" carried a lot of baggage straight into the conversation.

She tried to keep it light, nonetheless. "Yes?"

Evan turned his head toward her, but his face was unreadable. "Just so you know, I'm sorry for what happened. Particularly the way I treated you."

She had to swallow her shock. *That* certainly was the last thing she'd ever thought she'd hear. She'd given up hope of an explanation or apology years ago. "Thank you," she managed after a long pause.

He seemed genuinely surprised at her response. "For what?"

"For saying that. It means a lot."

He shrugged a shoulder as he changed lanes. "I know it doesn't change anything, but I can still regret my behavior. The apology may be years too late, but it is sincere."

It was oddly much easier to have this conversation side-on, instead of having to look directly at him. She kept her eyes front and said, *"For an admitted bastard, that was a nice apology."*

She cut her eyes toward him just in time to see the corner of his mouth twitch as if he found that funny. "Thank you."

I won't ask for details. Asking would sound pathetic and whiny. And there was a very good chance she wouldn't like what she would hear. "Can I ask why things ended the way they did between us?" she said, wincing even as she did.

"Beyond the fact I'm cold and selfish?"

This time, she did turn to face him. "You're saying there's *not* one?"

He looked at her as though he was sizing her up and coming to a decision. Then his eyes went back to the road as traffic began to move again. "Not that I'm willing to share."

"Like that's not going to drive me crazy now," she

muttered, really not caring what it might sound like to him.

"If I tell you it was genuinely me and not at all you, would that help?"

He sounded sincere, and something panged inside her, reminding her of the sweet side of him she'd seen and gone cow-eyed over in the past. Jory had been uncharacteristically closed-mouthed about Evan's background, but she'd known his childhood had been difficult and that he spent time at her parents' house because he was estranged from his own family. She easily painted him as wounded, and being naive and smug and influenced by too many romantic movies, she'd cast herself as the woman who'd heal the misunderstood bad boy's heart. "Maybe. But—"

A skater shot out in front of them, nearly invisible in the mist and dark, and Evan jammed on the brakes, throwing her against her seat belt. His hand flew out at the same time, landing painfully on her chest, and the effect of both managed to knock the breath out of her. The skater didn't even look back as he sped away.

Evan cursed, then asked, "You okay?"

"Yeah." She purposely looked down to where Evan's hand was still pressed against her chest, pretty much copping a feel. Evan moved his hand quickly, without comment *and* without the decency to look even a little abashed or surprised at where it ended up. She, however, felt branded, the imprint of his hand seeming to linger. In hindsight, she should have worn a bra tonight whether she needed it or not. "Dude has a death wish," she said to break the tension she felt even if he didn't.

"You were smart to walk. Traffic down here is abysmal."

"It'll clear some once you turn." The sudden stop had sent her purse into the floorboard, and she leaned over to gather the contents back up. Her lipstick, though, had rolled under the seat and she had to contort herself to get to it. Realizing the solution to both her physical and emotional situation, she gave one last stretch and got it, then sat up and said briskly, "I can walk from here, save you some time."

"Don't be ridiculous."

So much for that idea.

As she promised, the traffic was thinner on her street, and Evan pulled up in front of her building a minute later. "These are nice condos. I'm glad you're not doing the starving artist thing."

"I ate half a cow covered in cream sauce for dinner, so I think we've already covered the 'not starving' part," she said with a laugh. "And I have a roommate to help cover the rent. It's a great location for me. It's fifteen minutes on the bus to the studio, and I can walk pretty much everywhere else."

She had her purse over her shoulder and a hand on the door, and that horrible how-to-end-the-evening tension returned. Evan's face was partly shadowed and unreadable, giving her no help there. Not a date, not friends, not business associates.... She didn't know the protocol.

To her ever-loving surprise, Evan got out of the car and walked around to open her door. Her jaw was still hanging open as he extended a hand to help her out.

For someone who purported to be selfish, he'd been raised right when it came to good manners.

That shock, though, caused her to stumble as she climbed out, pitching herself straight into Evan's arms. He caught her easily, his arms strong and solid around her. He was warm, and damn it, he smelled good. Her heart jumped into her throat.

Over her head, she heard Evan chuckle. "That was graceful."

Kill me now.

He set her back on her feet. "You okay?" Evan asked.

"I'm fine. Just clumsy."

His eyebrow went up. "Maybe it was the wine."

"Yeah, maybe." Shaking it off, she rushed ahead with forced cheer and casualness. "Well, thanks again for dinner. And for the ride home."

His lips twitched. "Take care, Liv. And if you ever need anything, give me a call."

Oh, the irony. "Good night."

Evan waited until the security door closed behind her before driving away. It had been a really, really strange evening, where nothing had gone as planned, but it hadn't been bad either. The beginning and end hadn't been fantastic, but the middle part, like the over-dinner chitchat, had gone pretty well, all things considered. Had she not gone into it with a specific agenda, she'd have called the evening a success.

But even with that failure, the evening still wasn't a total disaster. She *did* live in the same city with Evan, and they might run into each other on occasion; having a truce in place made good sense. And when Jory came to town, he wouldn't feel as if he had to divide his time so precisely. *All good things*, she thought, as she climbed the last few stairs to her floor.

Everything else could just be ignored.

Annie was sprawled on the couch, flipping through TV channels, but she sat up when she heard her come in. "How'd it go?"

"Not bad."

"So he's going to sponsor you?"

"No."

"He turned you *down*? Jeez." Annie went to the counter and got a wineglass, filling it and handing it to her. "That sucks."

Olivia accepted the glass gratefully and sank into the cushions on the opposite end of the couch. "He didn't have to turn me down. I didn't ask."

"What? Why not?"

With a sigh, Olivia ran through the evening, all the small things that added up to tip the scales in the direction of keeping her mouth shut. She glossed over her rather disturbing reactions to him, because, for her own sanity, that was best left unexamined.

"I can't say I blame you. I see where you're coming from, and I'd probably feel the same way. But," Annie continued, as she cocked her head, "what, then, did you say to explain why you suddenly wanted to have dinner after all these years?"

"New in town, don't really know anyone…"

"Olivia, really?" Annie sighed. "He's going to think you still have the hots for him."

"What? No. Not likely."

"You said he has an ego."

"He does."

"Then he *will*. It's actually the only logical conclusion he could come to, to explain it."

"He might think I'm insane now, but that's about all." *And he might not be wrong.* She stood and handed her glass to Annie to finish. "I'm going to bed. I've got Pilates at eight tomorrow."

"I'm sorry it didn't work out."

"Me, too."

It was a shame, but there was always plan B. Plan B involved making sure that everyone from the chairman of the ballet board all the way down to the stagehands loved her *and* working her butt off to prove her value to the company. She'd also talk to the business office to see if they had any ideas of how she could land sponsorship—and to suss out how important that sponsorship really was.

That's what I should have done in the first place, she told herself as she got ready for bed. That was a far more sensible idea than a half-baked plan to talk Evan into it. Hell, plan B should have been plan A. Too bad she didn't think of it first.

At the same time, she didn't regret their meeting.

It would make things easier for Jory when he came to town. She didn't know exactly how much Jory knew about her and Evan, but her brother had made it very clear he considered his roommate off-limits to his little sister. He'd been unhappy and grumpy about it. She hadn't asked him to take sides, but he always seemed uncomfortable bringing up Evan around her after that, giving the whole thing a patina of awkward wrongness—at least to her mind. That, as much as anything else, had led to making it a *thing*—which, now at least, she realized it really didn't need to be.

So, in that sense, dinner wasn't such a bad idea, after all.

The wine, the food and a long day—both physically and mentally—were catching up with her, and the bed beckoned.

As she climbed in and pulled the covers up, she realized she'd gotten distracted by the near miss with that skater and hadn't followed up on his mysterious "genuinely me, not you" statement.

What could he have possibly meant?

The next morning, just outside Boca Raton, the sudden blaring of "Born This Way" caused Evan to swerve dangerously in his lane.

What the sweet hell? The news program chattered on from his car speakers, but that was undeniably Lady Gaga coming from…under the passenger seat?

Pulling off onto the shoulder, he searched under the seat until he found the source: a phone that went silent about the time he got hold of it. It had an overly sparkly rhinestone case, and when he pressed the home button to wake it up, Olivia and Jory smiled back at him.

He couldn't figure out how Olivia had managed to leave her phone in his car, but now the question was what to do with it. The screen had a long list of missed calls from "Annie" and "Theo." Presumably those calls were Olivia using her friends' phones to locate her own. But the phone was locked, so he had no way of calling back.

Based on the sheer volume of calls, though, if he waited another thirty minutes or so, Olivia would be calling again. Sliding the phone into his shirt pocket, he pulled back out onto the interstate.

Last night had certainly been odd. And while he still didn't have a good explanation for why Olivia had contacted him, he didn't regret it. He just wasn't sure what, if anything, it meant, and what, if anything, he should do about it.

It wasn't a feeling he liked. In fact, he intentionally avoided these kinds of situations. Everything needed to be up front and clear, without mystery or games or prevarications. Jory was a straight-up, no games, kind of guy, so he'd assumed Olivia would be the same. Why then did he feel so bothered at the idea she might not be?

He snorted. Maybe because he wasn't sexually attracted to Jory.

Of course, the next question was if Olivia was still attracted to him? He'd like to say yes, and there had been moments, but that could be wishful thinking on his part. But she had left her phone in his car...accidentally or intentionally?

He was pulling into the parking lot of Riley Construction when Olivia's phone rang again. "Hello?"

"Hi." There was great relief in her voice that didn't sound fake. "My name's Olivia, and you seem to have my phone."

Accidentally. That knowledge came with unexpected disappointment and made his words sharper than intended. "Because you left it in my car last night."

There was a pause, then a confused, "Evan?"

"Who else?"

"I thought I'd left it at the restaurant or something. I didn't even think to call you." He heard her sigh. "I'm *so* glad you have it, though. My life is in that phone."

"I know how you feel."

"We should be breaking for lunch soon. Can I meet you somewhere and get it?"

"I'm in West Palm Beach for a meeting and won't be back until later this afternoon."

"Oh." She sounded disappointed. "Well, let me know when and where would be good for you."

"I can drop it by the studio later, though, on my way home," he offered for some reason.

"That would be awesome. I'll be here until around five-thirty or so. The studio is in Wynwood."

"Then I can find it."

"Thanks, Evan. I really appreciate it."

He silenced the phone's ringer before putting it in

his briefcase. Although Olivia would quit calling her phone now, other people might, and he really didn't want that annoying song blaring out during the meeting. If he was remembering correctly, the MMBC studio wasn't too far out of his way home, and he could swing by easily.

But, jeez. She was at the studio already and would be there until five-thirty? When Olivia said she worked her body hard, she hadn't been kidding. Granted, he knew next to nothing about the subject, but he would have guessed the job would be part-time at best. How long could it take, really? He had to assume she knew all the moves; putting them in a specific order for a performance shouldn't take all *that* long.

She'd said yesterday that she'd been in rehearsals for six hours. He'd assumed that was either an exaggeration or at least unusual. Six or seven hours in a dance studio couldn't be easy, much less doing that every day. Or maybe she didn't dance the whole time? He had no idea. A six or seven hour workday didn't seem like much, but then Olivia wasn't exactly sitting at a desk.

Regardless of what his father might say, he wasn't averse to hard work. He'd nearly killed himself to get through school and graduated with enough debt to buy a decent-sized house. Honestly, it was one of the things he and Jory had first bonded over—although for different reasons. The Madisons weren't rich—their family restaurant in Tampa was popular, but hardly a gold mine—and Jory's work ethic was rooted in the love and support of a family that wanted him to succeed.

Neither Jory nor Olivia knew what it was like to drive themselves out of spite and desperation, but they drove themselves nonetheless.

He had to respect it.

Jory, though, had needed to learn to let go, to come out of his shell and trust his instincts. Evan liked to think he played a big part in that, even if it had been mostly through bad influence and serving as a cautionary tale from time to time. But being too serious, too focused and too sure had a downside—and all Evan had to do was point in the direction of his own family for an example.

On paper, his family sounded great; in practice, they were insufferable. He far preferred the Madisons; Jory had brought him home like a stray, and Gary and Dee showed him what real families could be—fun, accepting and loving without reservations or conditions. There was very little he wouldn't do for the Madisons. They'd probably saved him from himself.

Which was why he'd walked away when Jory asked him to—and why he'd done it the way he had. He didn't want to cause tension between Jory and Olivia. If Olivia had ever told her parents about it, Jory must've said something to keep him okay in their eyes. He'd taken the blame, been the jerk, hurt Olivia for her own good. But it had all seemed to work out.

But with Olivia back in his orbit, however tangentially at the moment, it made things a little complicated. Again.

He had a meeting in less than ten minutes and he

needed to focus. There was a lot of money riding on this pitch, and he couldn't risk blowing it because his brain was elsewhere. He wanted Riley Construction in his stable.

Three hours later, he had them. He emailed his assistant and his office manager the good news, then stripped off his tie, tossed it into the backseat, unbuttoned his collar and his cuffs, and put the top down for the ride home.

His brain was buzzing, high on the adrenaline rush of success and future plans, and he forgot he still needed to drop off Olivia's phone until he was almost past the exit.

The parking lot was much busier than he expected, packed with cars. He followed a very tall, very slender teenager and her mother to a set of glass doors and inside into an alternate dimension.

Dozens of young girls—from early tweens to just-licensed-to-drive—packed the hallway. All were tall and slim with their hair pulled severely back. They all wore black bodysuits and pink tights as they contorted themselves into various stretches. They looked like a small bun-headed robot army, ready to invade.

The noise was at a level painful to adult ears, with an occasional squeal rising above the din to make him wince.

He waded through the chest-high crowd, dodging swinging arms and flying feet, to a door marked Office. A middle-aged woman sat behind a desk, seemingly unconcerned with the melee right outside her door. "Can I help you?"

"I'm looking for Olivia Madison."

The woman was professionally distant. "She's in rehearsals. Can I help instead?"

"I'm Evan Lawford. I have her phone."

Her voice warmed immediately. "Oh, good. She mentioned you would be coming by. You're welcome to leave it here with me, and I'll see that she gets it. Or you can wait. They should be done in another fifteen minutes or so."

Wait? In that hallway of overly excited children?

The horror must have shown on his face, because the woman laughed. "*The Nutcracker* gives young dancers from the community the opportunity to perform with a professional company. It's a tradition, albeit a sometimes noisy one."

He reached in his pocket and handed over the phone. "I think I'll just leave the phone with you."

She winked at him. "Smart move. I can't say I blame you."

Back out in the hallway, he tried to move toward the door, but was blocked by adolescent Bun-Bots huddled in a pack near a large window he hadn't noticed on his way in.

None of them were taller than his shoulders, so he could easily see over their heads, and he wondered what was so attention-grabbing that it deserved their awe.

The window offered a side view into a studio with painted cinder block walls and a gray floor. Mirrors lined the front wall and metal bars were bolted to the other three. It was frankly depressing. A dark-haired man in street clothes gesticulated wildly with his hands, obviously trying to make a point to the two dancers standing in the middle of the room. The walls absorbed most of the sound, muffling the words but not the volume or the emotion behind them.

It took him a second to realize that the woman dancer was Olivia. Her hair was scraped back from her face, but small tendrils had worked themselves loose and clung to her face and neck—which were flushed pink from exertion.

She was wearing a one-piece black thing that clung to her like a second skin, emphasizing the long, clean lines of her torso and the length of her legs. Yes, she was thin, but street clothes had hid the truth of her body from him last night. At eighteen, she'd still been growing into herself, but now, Olivia was solid, sculpted muscle, more like an athlete than his mental picture of a dainty, fragile ballerina.

Both she and her partner—who had all of *his* attributes on display as well in just tights and a tank top—were dripping sweat. Yet neither of them seemed phased by the other man's enthusiastic diatribe; they both just nodded as he went over to a stereo and started the music.

Olivia took a breath and started to dance.

Seriously, the studio doors *had* to have been a portal to another dimension, as Olivia seemed able to defy the laws of gravity, physics *and* biomechanics.

She could spin like a dreidel on her toes, then melt into the arms of her partner, her back bent over his arm like her spine was made of rubber. Those long legs extended to impossible heights, her foot easily higher than her head, and her jumps would be the envy of NBA players and world-class hurdlers.

He found himself holding his breath as Olivia's partner lifted her high over his head, supporting her with only one hand in the small of her back. An impressed gasp rose from the crowd in front of him. He didn't blame them one bit.

It was truly the most amazing thing he'd ever seen the human body do, and Olivia did it all with a serene smile on her face, making it look easy and effortless.

Something heavy and hot landed in his stomach. He couldn't quite define it, but it was powerful and impossible to ignore. It was different than just desire: he'd wanted her nine years ago, and that want had nudged at him all last night, but this ran deeper, somehow.

He felt himself starting to sweat, and he left quickly, ending up in the front seat of his car. Seeing Olivia in action, even just for those few minutes, shifted his entire perspective about her.

Jory had said she was good, and he'd had no reason to doubt that, but this showed a side of Olivia he never really knew about. No one got that good at anything without hard work—*really* hard work, the kind few people, including himself, would ever experience or understand. He had to respect that level of determination and discipline. It made his own drive seem pale in comparison.

And Jory had been right to expect Evan to leave her alone. Their affair would have ended—and probably badly, too—in quick enough time, only Olivia would have ended up hurt worse. He knew himself too well, both then and now, to think he'd have been a positive influence in her life at that point.

He still wasn't much of a prize. All anyone had to do was ask any of the past ten women he'd dated, and they'd provide a long list of his flaws. Which, again, he was well aware of—and even if he hadn't been, those flaws had been listed for him repeatedly, usually at top volume mere moments before the woman stormed out.

He should walk away. Quickly and to a great distance.

But he wasn't sure if he wanted to. And he was not one to always do the right thing when the wrong thing held much more appeal.

And Olivia was definitely appealing.

CHAPTER THREE

Being separated from her phone all day had Olivia feeling twitchy and disconnected. Getting it back made her feel like a junkie who'd finally found a fix. Not that she'd really missed all that much, but it was the feeling she *could* have that caused detox jitters.

She wished she'd been able to tell Evan thanks in person; after all, he had gone out of his way to return it to her when she'd been silly enough to leave it in his car in the first place. That would just be good manners.

At the same time, it was probably easier this way. All things considered, she'd had a good time at dinner last night. Evan could be funny and quite charming when he wanted to; even with his assurances he was cold at heart. And she had to question her sanity at her willingness to appreciate that charm when he'd treated her so badly. It made her feel shallow, as if she was desperate and able to fall for good looks and flattery over substance.

It had always seemed strange to her that Jory could be so close to someone like Evan, and she'd been horrified to see Jory adopt some of Evan's partying and hell-raising ways, but Jory was a good man, and he wouldn't be friends with someone completely irredeemable.

And it *had* been a long time. She wasn't the same person she'd been nine years ago, so even with his denials to the contrary, Evan probably wasn't either.

Good grief, she was being ridiculous. She was either lonely or insane or sex-starved—or possibly a combination of the three. Why else would she be having this argument with herself?

Evan had dropped her off last night with "Call me if you need anything," which could be loosely translated as "Have a nice life," so it wasn't even an issue worth stressing over. To assuage her inner Miss Manners, though, she emailed him a quick, simple, "Thank you," and then pushed the whole thing out of her mind to protect her sanity.

She wasn't in a hurry, and there was no good reason to fight the masses on the bus during rush hour. So she showered, picked up her shoe allotment, checked the board for photo calls and rehearsal changes, and spoke to a few of the young girls waiting for their turn to rehearse—general dithering.

She'd make a quick trip to the grocery store for dinner supplies, then head home to an evening of TV and sewing.

It wasn't the most exciting of evenings, but her life didn't exactly suck, either. She'd signed on for this life, so she couldn't complain.

Outside the studio, she stopped to get a barrette

to pull her hair back. When she heard her name, she looked up.

Evan was leaned up against his car, arms crossed over his chest. It was so unexpected, she had to do a double take to make sure it was him, and even then she couldn't be sure he'd actually been the one to call her name. But there was no one else in the parking lot, and the chances of him waiting for someone else had to be pretty slim. She changed course and headed toward him.

Evan looked like an advertisement in a magazine. His collar was loose and his sleeves were rolled up, but it was very much the "businessman after hours" look. Expensive clothes, expensive sunglasses perched on his head, expensive car.

His hair was messy, as though he'd been driving with the top down, and just a hint of five o'clock shadow traced his jaw. *Hummina.* He was picture-perfect, and she wouldn't lie to herself by denying it wasn't working on her. A little shiver slid through her insides. Whatever he was selling, she might be convinced to buy.

Down, girl. She wasn't a naive eighteen-year-old anymore; she knew better. And she knew exactly *what* he was, too, but sadly, that wasn't the bucket of cold water her good sense might hope for. In fact, knowing made it *worse*. If she wanted to, she could walk, eyes wide open, right into that place where what he was willing to give met up with what she wanted to take—with no misunderstandings or heartaches this time.

That was a big *if*, though.

Frankly, her brain was twisted to even go there. Hadn't she *just* gotten all this sorted out in her head?

Guess not. Or at least not entirely.

He looked so good that her vanity kicked in. She was quite glad she'd showered, but she wished she'd known he was here so she could have spent a little more time on herself. Maybe at least dry her hair so it wasn't hanging damp and limp down her back.

She'd gotten her phone from the office *before* her shower. *Before* she'd dithered around in the studio. Which meant Evan had been waiting out here for a good half hour or more, at least.

She felt a little bad about that, but also a little flattered, too, and she smiled as she got closer. "Hey. Thanks for bringing me my phone."

"You're welcome. It must have fallen out when I had to dodge that skater last night."

"Yeah, probably. I didn't expect to see you to thank you in person, so I sent you an email."

"I saw it."

This was weird. Evan looked completely comfortable, at ease even, but the conversation felt awkward. Forced. Since he was standing here, though, she had to assume he had *some*thing to say to her, but there was no nice way to ask "What do you want?". Grasping for conversational straws, she said, "And thanks again for dinner. I had a nice time."

"I did, too. We should do it again."

Well, that was an improvement from the "have a nice life" feeling of last night. The wisdom of another dinner could be examined another time; right now, she'd take it as a compliment. "Sure."

"Are you hungry?"

Whoa. Okay. That was fast. "Now?"

"I watched rehearsals for a little bit. It looks like a good way to work up an appetite."

"Well, um…" She paused as the full statement registered. "You watched rehearsals?"

"Just for a few minutes. You're really good."

She examined his tone for flippancy and didn't find any. If anything, he seemed genuinely impressed. "Thanks."

"I don't know much—anything, actually—about it, but it was still pretty impressive."

She wasn't going to play with false modesty—she'd worked too hard for that—so there wasn't really much to say to that other than "Thank you" even if she'd already said it once.

"So *are* you hungry?"

She was, but…she gestured to her outfit. "I'm not really dressed to go anywhere."

He held up his phone. "According to Siri, there's a great deli-bistro-type place just a couple of blocks from here. I assume it's casual."

"Huey's? Yeah, it's a great place."

"Okay, then. Can we leave the car here?" She nodded, and he opened the trunk. "Then drop your stuff."

Flattery had given way to confusion and uncertainty. They had a past, but it was past. Was he just being friendly or was he hoping he might get lucky tonight?

Was it a little of both? Or neither? Or something else entirely? And why couldn't she decide where her feelings on those possibilities fell on the spectrum?

Oh, jeez. How could Evan mess with her head so easily? And what kind of fool was she to let him?

"Liv? Are you okay?"

She snapped her head up to see Evan standing next to his open trunk, his hand out waiting for her to hand him her stuff and a confused look on his face. "Yeah." She handed over her bags, and he locked them inside. "Thanks."

She took two steps, then stopped. This wasn't an ideal time or place, but it would have to do. "What are we doing?"

Evan looked at her as if she'd lost her mind. "Going to dinner? At least, that's what I thought we were doing."

"No. I mean, why? Why *now*? Considering…"

The confusion cleared and he nodded. "I could ask you the same thing. You're the one who made first contact."

He had her there. And she still didn't have a plausible alternative reason for why she did. "Maybe I didn't realize there'd be a second time."

"There doesn't have to be. I'm not going to drag you to the restaurant and force-feed you—even if you do look like you really need a sandwich."

"Evan, be serious."

"I am."

"Do you honestly believe there's nothing we need to discuss? No air to clear?"

Evan sighed, his face the perfect picture of resigned exasperation. "I feel I'm safe assuming the answer you're looking for is not 'yes.'" He shook his head. "I apologized. What more can I do?"

That was a good question, and one she should have answered for herself *before* asking him. She'd beat herself up over it, except Evan was far too good at scrambling her higher brain functions, turning her into a babbling idiot. "So we're going to be friends now?"

"I kind of thought that was the point of dinner last night."

Nothing ventured, nothing gained. "*Just* friends?"

"You're a beautiful woman, Olivia. Talented, smart, charming." He looked her up and down. "I'm not going to deny there's still an attraction."

"So not just friends, then?" Why did that possibility send a little thrill through her?

"That would be entirely up to you." The wicked little half smile held a challenge and that didn't help.

"And if I did want to be just friends?"

"I'd respect that." He thought about it for a second. "It'd be a novel experience for me."

"You're saying you don't have any platonic female friends?"

"I don't have many friends period."

She could relate to that, but still… "So you're telling me you've slept with every woman you know."

He grinned. "Not *all* of them. Some of them are married."

"You are insufferable."

He grinned. "So I've been told."

She felt off balance. "And this is supposed to encourage me?"

"Nope. I'm just being honest."

How could she be annoyed and intrigued at the same time? In fact, it was almost a challenge. But Evan *was* charming, and hadn't she decided that a peaceful coexistence with him would be a benefit all around?

"So are we going to dinner or not?" he asked.

She had to think about it for a minute. She needed to give herself the chance to weigh the pros and cons and decide if she wanted to shake things up a little bit. Because she had a suspicion that being in Evan's orbit—in whatever way—would not be boring. And now she understood what had drawn her bookish brother into his orbit, as well. The man was just irresistible—and not just in a sexual way. His attitude could be grating, but it was refreshing. And his ego, while quite large, made him fun to spar with. And while *she'd* had a problem with Evan and Jory's friendship, Jory never had, which said a lot about Evan as a person, giving clues to facets of his personality she wasn't aware of.

Oh, she might regret this later, but she might not, either. She might decide that they, too, could be friends, and it would be nice to have another friend. If she wanted to cross that line later? Well, she'd know what she was doing. And if, in the process of this new friendship, she decided that Evan was still a jerk, she could get out easily enough.

She nodded, trying to look regal and haughty—which was a little difficult when wearing yoga pants and a T-shirt with wet, wild hair. "We are."

"Then let's go."

Had he really just agreed to be just friends with Olivia? Considering the rather adult nature of his thoughts recently, that bordered on insane. But that seemed to be Olivia's choice. Could he keep her at arm's length? Maybe being friends would make the attraction wane.

Or not, he thought as he watched the sway of her hips as she walked. While Olivia was elegant, she also had a girl-next-door wholesomeness about her—especially right now, barefaced, uncoiffed and yet comfortable in her skin. Normally, that wasn't an attraction for him, but on Olivia it worked. A little *too* well. Oh, he'd created a challenge for himself. He'd have to play this carefully by ear with the full knowledge he might regret it later.

The MMBC studios occupied a converted warehouse on the fringe of the Wynwood Arts District. Wynwood was still primarily a mecca for the visual arts, but the performing arts were getting a toehold in the area, too. He wasn't overly familiar with the district, but Olivia seemed to be, and she pointed out items of interest as they walked. She was passionate about the arts in general, not just dance it seemed, as well as very knowledgeable, and she told him about shows and upcoming artists and the growth of the area.

"That looks like graffiti, not art," he said as she showed him a mural she claimed was a favorite.

"It can't be both?"

"I want to say no, but I'm starting to think that's not the correct answer."

She laughed.

"You must think I'm an uncultured troglodyte."

After a long pause that bordered on offensive, she finally answered. "Troglodyte? No. Uncultured? Maybe." The mock-haughty tone and twitching lips took the sting out of her words.

"You'll have to pardon me then, and blame it on my childhood. There wasn't much in the way of what you'd consider culture of any kind in Arrowwood, Florida."

"What does that have to do with anything? Beyond being an argument for improved arts education in Florida public schools, that is."

Looking pointedly at a sculpture that looked like salvaged bedsprings from a fairy's junkyard, he said, "I'm thinking art may be something that you have to grow up with to truly appreciate."

She shook her head. "No, it's not. It's for everyone. You just have to expose yourself to it. You don't always have to understand it to appreciate it for what it is. As you learn more about it, the more esoteric stuff will start to make sense. But something is bound to speak to you, if you give it time and the chance to."

"Since I'm reevaluating my mind-set about ballet, I just might believe you."

"That's very flattering." She grinned and it lit up her entire face. "I'd be happy to help you in your quest to expose yourself to what's out there. What do you think of this?"

The bedsprings? "It's um…interesting?"

"See, you're becoming more cultured even as we stand here."

"You know, I feel it." He put a hand to his chest dramatically. "It's like a flower blossoming in my heart, filling me with color and joy and wisdom all at the same time. This piece…it shows the waste and futility of society while celebrating the, the *resilience* of um, *springiness*. And purple."

"Smart ass." She shook her head as she led him away from the sculpture. "So where is Arrowwood, anyway?"

"North of Ocala, south of Gainesville, middle of nowhere."

"And your family is still there?"

"Yep." He didn't elaborate, hoping she wouldn't ask.

"Do you get to go home often?"

"No." It came out sharper than he intended. He could tell by the look in her eyes that Olivia caught the hint that time, and while she gave him an odd look, she didn't press further. The ensuing silence was a bit awkward and noticeable after the easiness of the conversation before, and he needed to find another topic before it either got worse or Olivia decided to ask more questions. Thankfully, he found it quickly. "Hey, look at that."

That was a poster-sized advertisement for *The Nutcracker*, featuring a full-color picture of Olivia in a white-and-silver tutu and tiara. The man holding her up looked vaguely as if he might have been the same man she had been dancing with earlier. "Good picture. Cool pose."

Olivia looked a little embarrassed. "Thanks. That's a fish."

"You're a fish? I thought it was a Christmas-type story."

"It is." She laughed. "That *move* is called a fish, but I'm the Snow Queen—in that picture, at least."

He was getting more confused, not less. "So you're *not* the Snow Queen?"

"Oh, I'm the Snow Queen, but I'm also a mother in the party scene and I alternate Sugar Plum Fairy and Arabian in the second act."

"Is that all?"

He meant that as snark, but it seemed it wasn't. "I also had to learn Dew Drop, just in case, but I wouldn't do them all in the same show." Olivia also must have misunderstood the look in his face, too, as she quickly added, "*Nutcracker* is a big show and we're not that big of a company. I'm just lucky we have a large enough corps to cover Waltz and Snow."

Very few of her words made sense, but her tone was easy enough to understand. "You don't sound very excited about the show."

She shrugged. "It's *Nutcracker*. There's no escaping it."

"Escaping?"

"Almost every ballet company does *Nutcracker* at Christmas. It's a tradition, and because so many people consider it part of their Christmas tradition, it makes a lot of money in ticket sales. So that's great and all, and I'm so glad people love it so much, but you have to understand—this is my twentieth year doing this ballet."

Twentieth? His jaw fell open a little bit, causing her to grin.

"When I was eight, I went with a friend to *Nutcracker* auditions in Tampa, even though I'd never set foot in a studio before at that point. I was cast as a Bon Bon in act 2, and all I really had to do was skip around the stage and look cute. I was hooked, though, from that moment on, and my folks enrolled me in ballet classes in the January. I have danced *Nutcracker* someplace on this planet every single year since then."

"Wow."

"Exactly. I did the math once, and when you consider that rehearsals for a December show start in late September or early October, I've spent nearly five *years* of my life preparing for and dancing in that one show." She leaned in and whispered, "Don't spread this far and wide, but I'm kinda over it."

"But…"

She raised an eyebrow at him. "Are you going to tell me that there's *no* part of your job that you don't find boring or monotonous or frustrating? Or wouldn't be after you'd done that one thing for five solid years?"

There were plenty, but he didn't call himself an *artist*, dedicated to his craft. "No, but—"

She lifted her hands as if to say *there you go* and opened the door to the restaurant.

"Wait a second." He motioned her back from the door. "You're telling me you don't enjoy it?"

"Dancing? Yes. Performing? Yes. *Nutcracker?* That gives me hives. Just hearing the music is enough to make me start to twitch, and it's *everywhere* this time of year."

"If your marketing and PR people knew how you felt, they'd put a gag order on you before they let you out in public."

"Hey, now, I can behave in public." As if to prove that, Olivia lifted her head and in an interview-perfect tone said, "I'm so thrilled to be making my first appearance in MMBC's production of this classic and timeless ballet. It's truly a Christmas tradition, enjoyable for people of *all* ages, and I encourage *every*one in town to come see the show."

"That's better," he admitted as Olivia grinned at him again. No one would be able to tell she hadn't been grumbling about it five seconds before. "You're a good liar."

"I'm not lying," she protested. "Every word of that was true."

"You're good at lies of omission, then." A strange look crossed Olivia's face, and he wondered if he'd insulted her somehow. "But I respect that. I'm in advertising, remember? It's all about the image." He opened the door to the restaurant and motioned for her to go in. "Now let's eat."

Olivia's order tonight was far more in line with what he'd expect—a hummus and veggie pita with a side of fruit and iced tea. "I can't eat like I did last night *all* the time," she explained with a shrug. Then, over his protests, she insisted on buying both their dinners. "If we're going to be friends, you can't buy all the time either."

Evan couldn't quite find his balance in all of this. Olivia's grudge had somehow been appeased, but he still felt as if he was on probation with her—regardless of her easy, friendly attitude. It was the quick switch that bothered him. People didn't just adapt like that.

But he saw no danger in enjoying it, as long as he didn't forget who she was.

And there was no danger of *that*.

CHAPTER FOUR

TONIGHT WAS EASIER by far than last night, Olivia thought. Having an understanding—even if she didn't fully understand it—with Evan helped, and she was actually able to relax. His very bald "it's up to you" kept a flirty undercurrent running under the dinner conversation that was actually kind of fun.

Plus, after watching that little bit of rehearsals, Evan suddenly had an interest in ballet and peppered her with questions.

"Have you ever been dropped?" Evan had a keen interest in the lift he'd seen.

"Yes. But not ever from that particular lift and never by Theo."

"So you trust him."

"With my life." She laughed. "I've known Theo since we were really young. He was my partner when we took silver at Nationals. We've done thousands of lifts together."

"But you *have* been dropped before."

"Of course. It's not fun, but it does happen. I even

ended up with a mild concussion once." She took one last sip of her drink and started cleaning up the debris of their meal.

Evan wasn't quite letting it go, though. "You say that like it's nothing."

"It was an accident. Like I said, it happens. Sometimes it's something I did, sometimes it's something he did, but there's no sense assigning blame. You learn from it and go on."

"And if you get hurt?"

"You're much less likely to make that mistake again, that's for sure. But it's his job to do his best to catch me before I hit the floor. Partners who goof around and make it more likely someone's going to fall will soon find themselves without partners at all."

"Are there men you won't dance with?"

She nodded. "But most of the time, I just do what I'm supposed to do and trust my partner to do his part." She stood. "You ready?"

Evan stood, too, and led her toward the door. "But to let some guy hold you upside down with one hand? That's a lot of trust."

"It goes both ways, you know. If I mess up, he could get hurt. I could injure his back or his shoulders or kick him in the head. Or he could get hurt trying to keep *me* from getting hurt from something that was my own fault." It was fully dark outside now, cool, but not cold, and the neighborhood's nightlife was warming up. "We have to trust each *other*, or else we'll both end up hurt."

"How very Zen of you," Evan scoffed, as he fell into step beside her, adjusting his pace to hers.

"I know it sounds cheesy, but it's the truth."

"Trust has to be earned," he said seriously, causing her to do a double take at the emotion in his voice. Before she could answer though, he continued. "It takes time. You just show up and trust that this guy is not going to drop you on your head."

"That's not how it works."

"No?"

"Of course not. It's like sex."

It was a common joke in the studio, and she said it without really thinking how Evan might interpret it. When he stumbled, then looked at her with wide eyes, she regretted saying it. But when he reached for her elbow and pulled her out of the flow of foot traffic next to a Picasso-inspired mural to ask, "*Sex?*" she lost the regret. *This might be fun.*

She couldn't quite name the look on his face—horrified interest? shocked interest?—but it was enough to spur her on. "Just like you shouldn't jump into bed with someone you just met, you don't introduce yourself to a new partner and then do the most complicated lift in the program." She tried to put the right amount of earnestness into her words. "It would be all awkward, you know, feet and hands in all the wrong places, and getting frustrated because it's not feeling right and it's not any good for either one of you. And what's the point of having sex if you're not going to enjoy it? Sex is great, but good sex is *better*, and *great* sex takes an investment. *That* kind of great sex requires a little trust in your partner."

Evan cleared his throat and Olivia felt wicked.

"So you start slow and simple, feeling each other out." She ran a hand lightly over his chest. "You look for quirks that you'll need to adapt to and learn how his body moves." She ran her hands up his arms and squeezed his biceps gently. *Wow.* "You have to find your partner's strengths, learn how his hands feel, and how you'll fit together…that's the foreplay. And you can't rush that, can you?" Evan shifted uncomfortably as she moved her hands up and over his shoulders, but he shook his head. She leaned in, lowering her voice, moving slowly around his body, trailing her fingers. "You've got to get in sync with your partner first, and then…*then* you can trust him to do what needs to be done. *Then y*ou're free to go at it hard, full-out, over and over, until you're sweaty and exhausted, but satisfied with what you accomplished. And that feels *amazing*."

Evan's breath had gotten shallow as she spoke. More surprisingly, so had hers. She dropped her hand as Evan swallowed hard and gave himself a small shake. "You are evil, Olivia Madison."

"Whatever do you mean?" she protested with as much eyelash-fluttering innocence as she could muster.

When Evan lifted his eyes to hers, she saw heat there. It fanned embers she'd been trying to smother, and they flared with an intensity that rocked her back on her heels. Regretting she'd let bravado lead her into the deep end, she stepped back to let some air between them. The option may have been put out there, but she wasn't ready to decide whether to exercise that option or not.

But Evan certainly looked ready. And, *damn*, that was tempting. "So, anything else you want to know about ballet?" She tried for a light and airy tone and started walking again. "Pointe shoes? Tutus? Turns?" she tossed over her shoulder as Evan caught up.

"As a matter of fact, I do have more questions."

"Ask away."

"I'm curious about positions. Beyond the basics, of course." An eyebrow went up in challenge. "And what about your flexibility? Stamina?"

Jeez, she really was in over her head. She should know better than to play games with a master. "What about them?"

They were back at Evan's car, where her stuff was in his trunk. Figuring he'd have one of those fancy keyless entry things, she reached for the trunk latch and was rewarded when it popped open. Grabbing her bag, she tossed it over her shoulder and turned to face him. *Big mistake.* Evan was close. *Very* close. She could smell him, feel the heat of his body. And she was trapped between him and his stupid fancy car.

His smile was wicked. "Or you could just tell me more about that foreplay."

Over his shoulder, she could see her bus arriving like a gift from God to get her out of this. She focused on the relief of that and tried to ignore the little shiver that went through her. "Another time, maybe." She shimmied out and ran toward the bus stop, hand up to signal the driver to save her simply by stopping. "Bye!"

She looked back over her shoulder as she climbed aboard, only to see Evan leaned against the trunk of his car, grinning at her. When he saw her looking, he shouted, "Coward!"

Maybe so, but I'm not stupid, too.

Surprisingly enough, Olivia got in touch a few days later with an invite to something called "Margaritas and Melodies," which turned out to be a fundraiser for the symphony. She was taking his arts education seriously, it seemed.

He'd been torn, unable to decide, when her invite first landed in his in-box. He recognized danger when he saw it.

He might have agreed to just being friends, and she might be on board for that, but it was going to be very hard. He wanted her; he wouldn't lie to himself about that, but *three* outings? He either needed to nip this in the bud, or accept the direction this was heading and the possible consequences of that.

He wanted to be a better person and a good friend to Jory, but his big head wasn't exactly in total control. He'd accepted the invite before he'd really thought it all the way through and now, here he was—consequences or no consequences.

It was a casual affair, held in one of the larger galleries in the art district. They had a good-sized crowd packed in there, and the conversations nearly drowned out the background music of the symphony playing pop tunes given a classical twist. There were the usual fundraiser things—silent auctions, raffles, light refreshments and an overpriced cash bar.

He knew a lot of the people in attendance, though, and all of them seemed surprised to see him there. It was a good place to make new business contacts. He should have gotten more involved in the arts sooner.

He mentioned that to Olivia, and she gave him a pitying look. "I can't believe you're just now figuring that out. But," she corrected sternly, "you're not here to do business. You're supposed to be absorbing the atmosphere and appreciating the culture."

"The music is nice."

"It is. Our symphony is great and we're lucky to have that talent here. What do you think of the art?"

Frankly, he found it garish and ugly, as if the artist had randomly stuck household trash to a canvas and flung paint at it. "It's…unusual."

"I think it's hideous," she whispered.

"Wait, what? It's art."

"Yes, it's art, but that doesn't make it *good* art. The value in the piece often lies in the eye of the beholder, but I think it's derivative, amateurish and ugly." She leaned in to read the artist's name. "And this Jackson Pollack wannabe is…Damien Hoffman. Ever heard of him?"

"No."

"Looking at this stuff, I'm surprised anyone has."

"I thought you artsy types stuck together. Feeling the muse and all that jazz."

"I work really hard to perfect what I do. This guy rolled out of bed, stuck rubber bands to a canvas, called it art and had the nerve to slap a two-thousand-dollar price tag on it." Olivia sounded personally insulted.

"Ooh, do I hear some interdisciplinary infighting? Paintbrushes versus pointe shoes at dawn," he teased.

She cleared her throat. "The music is nice, though."

"So we said. Here, have a snack. You're getting grumpy." He offered her his plate, piled high with bite-size hors d'oeuvres.

"No, thank you."

"It's not bad stuff."

She wrinkled her nose. "That's okay."

"First you insult the art and now the food? *Tsk, tsk.*"

"If I'm going to load up on carbs and fat and calories, I'm going to go get a piece of cheesecake from the bakery and really make it worth my while. Not all junk food is created equal, and I'm picky about my splurges." She smiled. "But I will take another margarita."

"That, I can handle." He tossed the plate and offered her his arm. They headed toward the bar, only to be waylaid by a couple of his clients.

When they finally got past, she said, "You seem to know a lot of people here."

"I've lived in Miami for six, nearly seven years now. It happens."

"Since so many of them seem to be plugged-in to

the arts community, I'm surprised your friends haven't dragged you to these kinds of things long before now."

"Oh, man, I'm going to be on every mailing list in the city now, aren't I?"

She nodded without sympathy. "Yep. That's what friends are for."

"I know them," he explained, "but I wouldn't say we're friends."

She nodded. "That I understand."

"Really?" Olivia seemed friendly and outgoing. She shouldn't have a hard time making friends. Jory certainly didn't, so he assumed it was just part of the Madison DNA. "I don't like a lot of people. What's your excuse?"

"I just don't normally stay in one place long enough to make a lot of friends."

"You sound like you're on the run from the law or something."

"I have commitment issues," she confessed matter-of-factly. "I've never been able to agree to anything that locks me in longer than a season. And even then, I have small panic attacks before I sign the contract."

"I'm not sure that's healthy. Have you talked to a psychiatrist?"

"I'm not crazy." He looked unconvinced, so she added, "At least not in any clinical sense, thank you very much. But see, when I was accepted into the National Ballet Academy, I realized dance was what I really wanted to do with my life, and I began to believe I could actually make it my career. So, I made a list of all the places in the world I wanted to dance and all the things I wanted to achieve. I've been checking that list off ever since."

"Like where?"

"New York, Boston, San Francisco, London, Paris, Rome, Prague—"

"Prague?"

She nodded. "Great city. They have wonderful support for their ballet companies."

And he'd lived in Florida his entire life. "You're quite the traveler."

"Jory says I have itchy feet, and it's true. I do."

"That's got to be tough, though."

"It can be. It's got its problems, but it makes up for it in other ways. This is the life I chose, and I don't regret it. I've gotten to see and do a lot."

But there was a cost to everything, he knew. "What's your record?"

"My second time in New York. I stayed eleven months, but only because I stayed on to do summer stock."

"And the shortest?"

"Honolulu, six years ago," she answered immediately. "I signed a six-month contract, but broke my foot three weeks after I got there, and they released me from it. I knew some folks in Dallas, so I went there to recuperate and finished out the season with their company as a guest artist once I was well."

He ordered their drinks. "I didn't hear Miami on that list."

"It wasn't, but priorities shift as you get older. I'm ready to slow down a little, start looking ahead to retirement and what happens after that."

The absurdity of that made him laugh. "You're talking about retirement while everyone else your age is just starting their careers."

"Yes, but that gives me the chance to do something completely different if I want—I don't even have to stay in the arts. I could go school and learn about…" she said with a grin, "advertising, maybe."

"I don't recommend it."

"You seem to be doing pretty well."

"Exactly. The Lawford Agency would crush your little upstart biz like a bug." He handed her the drink and lifted his in a mock toast.

"How very pleasant of you."

"Hey, you're not the only one who made a list of things they wanted to accomplish."

"Really? What's on yours?"

"The only one you need to worry about is number two—making my agency the biggest and best in Miami."

"What's number one?"

"Making it the biggest in the world."

"Oooh, I like a man with big plans. Why don't—"

He didn't hear the rest of that statement because he caught sight of Elaine headed toward him like a missile. *Hell.* He hauled Olivia up against his side, ignoring her shocked "What on earth…?" as he anchored an arm around her waist.

"Evan." Although Elaine was pretending to be friendly, she lacked control over her tone of voice.

"Elaine."

"You're the last person I expected to see here."

"Well, I'm full of surprises."

Elaine looked at Olivia expectantly, and Olivia seemed to finally understand the situation, relaxing into him and smiling at Elaine.

"I don't believe I know your friend."

"This is Olivia Madison. She dances with the Miami Modern Ballet Company. Liv, this is Elaine MacDonald. Elaine's a software designer."

Olivia extended her hand. "Lovely to meet you."

"I'm afraid I don't follow the ballet. It's so old-fashioned at times, and I prefer my arts more modern and cutting-edge." Elaine was taking out her jealousy and hostility toward him by insulting Olivia, who didn't deserve it. He bristled.

"Well, ballet's not for everyone," Olivia answered quickly. Although she'd said almost exactly the same thing to him, her tone was different, landing the insult easily, yet without sounding like it. He was impressed, and waited to see where Olivia would go next.

"I prefer the visual arts," Elaine explained condescendingly. "For instance, I've been following Damien's career since the beginning. The energy and innovation in his work is so exciting," she gushed in the direction of the paintings. "It's very avant-garde, and not for everyone."

Olivia nodded in agreement. "I agree it's not for

everyone, because its over-derivative nature shows an immaturity in the artist that concerns me—or maybe it's just a lack of knowledge." She turned to Evan and smiled sweetly again. "What's coming out of New York right now in this medium is incredible. I guess it just hasn't made it to Miami yet."

Boom. That was a direct hit and Elaine's face reddened. Maybe she would think twice next time before picking a fight with someone who didn't deserve it.

Or maybe not. Elaine was taking a deep breath. And he stepped in before things got really ugly. "Good to see you, Elaine, but we must be off. Take care." He steered Olivia to the other side of the room. "I'm liking this friend thing," he whispered in her ear.

"Do you want to tell me why I just got in an Art 101 competition with that woman?"

"Because you are amazing and delightful and I could kiss you right now. That was brilliant and Elaine totally deserved it."

"But I didn't," she reminded him.

"I know, and I'm sorry. That was her way of trying to needle me."

"What did you do to her?"

He hesitated.

"*Oh,*" Olivia said, nodding as understanding dawned. "If I'd known *that*, I might not have taken her down like that. After all, I understand where she's coming from."

"It's not the same thing at all. I mean, you just met her. She's not a nice person."

"But you slept with her anyway?"

He could see her estimation of him sliding south even as she spoke. "I didn't know she wasn't a nice person when I did," he said in his own defense.

"I see. But still…"

"It would be one thing for her to take it out on me because I can handle it and I possibly even deserve it."

"*Possibly?*" Olivia snorted and rolled her eyes.

He cleared his throat. "But attacking another woman just because I might be sleeping with her now? That's bad form."

"You should be more careful about the women you get involved with, then."

"We weren't 'involved,'" he corrected. "We went out a few times."

"And you slept together."

"Well, yes. She's beautiful, and I promise I didn't know she was crazy at the time."

"So you were keeping everything casual."

"Yep. Always do."

"And she didn't know that?"

"Guess not."

Olivia cocked her head. "Why?"

"Why didn't she know? Beats me."

"No," she corrected gently, "why do you keep everything casual?"

"So many questions. What difference does it make?" Olivia just stared at him. Finally, when he couldn't stand the silence another second, he said, "Because I make a terrible boyfriend. Ask any of my exes."

"At least you admit it. That's the first step, you know, admitting you have a problem."

"Oh, I'm selfish, unable to commit…"

"Egotistical, a womanizer, smug…" she supplied.

"Gee, thanks."

"If we're going to be friends, I have to be able to be honest with you," she said primly.

"Maybe I should rethink this friend thing," he muttered.

"The truth hurts." She patted his arm. "But think of all the opportunity you have for personal growth. Then you can have a real relationship one day."

"Oh, you're one to talk."

Olivia's mouth fell open. "I beg your pardon?"

"I don't see you in a relationship."

"I told you. I move around a lot. That, in and of itself, is an issue," she explained, "but I'm also very committed to what I do. I love my job and it comes first. A lot of guys can't handle that."

"We're both just doomed to be forever alone, then, huh?"

"Yeah." She sighed. "It's a good thing we're pretty."

He looked at her and they both burst out laughing.

"Come on," he said, "Let's get out of here. I've had enough culture for one evening."

"And I'm hungry," she added.

"Why am I not surprised?" At least he could let go of any worries he might have about her eating habits. "The pigs in a blanket would have at least filled you up, you know."

"Yuck. There's another place I like about three blocks from here. Will you eat falafels?"

Ugh. "Art *and* falafels in one night?"

"Yes. Good brain food and good body food."

He sighed. "Fine. If I must."

She sighed and took pity on him. "There's a pizza truck just down from the falafel place."

"Then lead on."

About a block later, he remembered what else he wanted to ask. "By the way, what *is* going on in the New York art scene right now?

She shot him a look that questioned his sanity. "How the hell would I know? I'm a ballet dancer."

He burst out laughing. This friend thing…it wasn't always easy to remember just to be friends, but it wasn't as bad as he thought it would be, either.

But then, Olivia had never been what he expected anyway.

And he liked that.

A couple of days went by and Olivia didn't hear from Evan at all. She couldn't decide if that was a good thing or not. It was probably the *wise* thing, but still….

They were friends, and those weren't dates, so it wasn't like he owed her a follow-up call. At the same time, there'd been those *moments* which made the lack of contact now seem like a rejection. So while lack of contact seemed the wiser option, it didn't feel like the better option and bordered on slightly insulting.

Evan—or actually his agency's page, but still—had

liked her Facebook page, and she'd returned the "like," but that meant less than nothing.

It was all too weird. Annoying. Of course, then she got annoyed at herself for being annoyed in the first place. So juvenile.

This was definitely a sign that she needed a group, a posse, something. The lack of a large social circle wasn't new for her—because she moved around a lot, she tended to have more acquaintances than actual friends—but the disappointment over it *was* new. Maybe it was because she really did want to put down roots here, and knowing *that* made her more aware of the sparseness of her life in general.

She owned no furniture—another reason why she'd chosen to live with a roommate in a furnished apartment—and very little "stuff." She'd moved her entire life to Miami from Chicago in a rented Subaru Forester with room to spare. Memorabilia and keepsakes and that kind of stuff had always lived in a rental shed in Tampa, waiting for the day she'd settle down or retire.

If Miami was going to be that place, then she needed to start building a life here—one beyond the studio. It was a little scary to contemplate, and the fact she was annoyed at Evan of all people drove home how much she needed to just commit and get started on that. She'd been here three months already; what was her excuse? *Beyond* the niggling worry that her contract wouldn't be renewed next season. She'd never been without a job or an offer before; she wasn't going to be unemployed.

Maybe the fact she wanted this so much was driving the fear she wouldn't get it.

But she also knew that worry was just asking for failure. *If you worry you will fall, you will fall.* It was advice she'd passed on to hundreds of young dancers—and it was *good* advice. She needed to listen to her own platitudes.

She'd just have to work under the assumption that everything would work out the way she wanted and that Miami would become home. The worst-case scenario? She'd have to rent a bigger truck when she moved.

So by Friday, she'd made her first major purchase, and she luxuriated with her laptop on the wonder that was a new mattress and bedding and surfed the internet in well-supported, high-thread-count comfort. She felt oddly grown up.

She'd given up on wondering what kind of friends she and Evan were supposed to be, so she was quite surprised when her phone rang and Evan's name popped up on the screen. "Hey."

"How've you been, Liv?"

"Good. Busy as always. You?"

"The same."

They were the masters of inanity. And she was getting the feeling that Evan did it on purpose, just to throw her off balance. But for someone who'd been wondering if or when Evan was going to call, she was remarkably without a topic of conversation. "So what's up?"

"Do you work tomorrow?"

"I've got rehearsals until three, why?"

"Would you like to go to a party tomorrow night?"

She needed a minute to process that question. Dinner was different than a party. Dinner was simply food, and people had to eat. She was helping Evan expand his arts education. They could make as much or as little out of those as they needed. A party with his friends was a whole other animal. That might be an actual "date" and did she want to go there?

Evan had to be a mind reader because he seemed to pick up on the thoughts whirling through her mind. "It's a business thing. One of my clients is having their holiday party early to beat the after-Thanksgiving rush, and it's so much easier if I bring a date."

So it was a date, but not a "date." She wasn't sure how she felt about that.

She started to ask how a date would make it easier for him, but stopped herself before she asked the single most ignorant question ever. Evan was young, good-looking, successful and single. "So, in reality, you need a beard."

He laughed. "More like a shield."

"Do I get combat pay?" she teased.

"Free food and booze—and this client goes all out, so it should be quality food and booze. Well worth the splurge."

"While I do the arm-candy-small-talk-thing? Um...I don't know."

"One, while I'm sure you'll make great arm candy,

don't feel you need to hang on mine every second of the evening. Two, Matt Abrams is a big supporter of the arts scene, so between him and his family, friends and clients, there's a good chance you'll find some arty and cultured people there to talk to."

That got her attention. "Matt Abrams as in the Abrams Corporation?"

"Yes. Why? Is that a problem?"

The Abrams family were like gods in the Miami arts and humanities scene. A concert series, a lecture series and an entire *wing* of the art museum carried their name. The MMBC ballet board genuflected at the mere mention of the family. They were already donors, of course, but meeting and mingling in a social situation—well, it wouldn't hurt her to be personally known by any of them.

And, a little voice reminded her, she was still in need of a sponsor. An Abrams corporate event *had* to be a good place to find one.

"Olivia?"

She'd been spinning too long again. Evan was going to think she was mentally deficient in some way. "Formal or semiformal?"

"Cocktail is fine. Do you have a dress?"

"Of course."

"Then I'll pick you up around seven-thirty."

"I'll be ready."

Hanging up, she gave herself a congratulatory mental pat on the back. Seems she hadn't been making such bad choices, after all. Her reward for not being tacky

and asking Evan for the sponsorship was entry into
the very social circle that could provide exactly that.

Being Evan's friend definitely had benefits.

CHAPTER FIVE

OLIVIA WAS A HIT at the Abrams's party, and Evan congratulated himself on his excellent idea. She was elegant and charming, mingling easily with the other guests and a whiz at party small talk. She'd confessed in the car on the way over that meet and greets were as much a part of her repertoire as *Swan Lake*, as they were essential for…*something*. He hadn't been paying as much attention as he should have because Olivia in a little black sparkly number had fried much of his brain. A simple back sheath that looked demure from the front dipped low in the back to show the sculpted muscles of her shoulders and the long line of her spine from her upswept hair to the small of her back. The hem stopped high enough on her thigh to showcase those amazing legs without looking trashy. Although he'd managed to get his tongue off his toes—eventually—every now and then he'd catch sight of her unexpectedly and all his blood would rush south again.

He wasn't sure he'd be able to hold up his end of this "friends" deal—simply because he couldn't guarantee he'd be able to keep his hands off her for much longer. Not and keep his sanity intact, too. He had to be a masochist to even consider it. Olivia's uneven, hot-and-cold flirting was an added stumbling block, as he couldn't quite tell where her thoughts were heading.

But tonight, they were here as "friends," and repeatedly introducing her and explaining their relationship—"my best friend's sister"—*should* be enough of a reminder to keep his hands in his pockets. But since he rarely brought women to business events, questions about the true nature of their relationship were clear in everyone's eyes.

It was probably in his, too.

Olivia didn't require constant attention, which was nice, allowing him to socialize and mix business in as needed. These people were potential new clients for his agency, and he needed to work the room. But she was also usually near enough to function as that all-important shield, keeping enough speculation alive to prevent any other women from making their move.

A couple of hours into the evening, Matt Abrams made his speech, thanking everyone for another great year. Then the band started playing and people headed for the dance floor.

Olivia was chatting with a woman he vaguely recognized as the wife of one of the city managers as he sidled up beside her. They exchanged pleasantries for a few minutes, then the woman made her excuses with a smile and left them alone.

"Having a good time?"

"I am. Thanks for bringing me. And you were right—the food is great."

He hadn't seen her go near the buffet, but that was neither here nor there. Olivia was also going easy on the booze, nursing a glass of champagne while others were starting to feel their buzzes. When he offered to get her another, she shook her head. "I'd rather stay sober. I don't want to make a fool of myself in front of all these people."

He inclined his head toward the dance floor. "Then why don't we go dance?"

Olivia shook her head. "I said I *didn't* want to make a fool of myself."

"No one's expecting any fancy moves out of you, Twinkletoes."

"Well, that's good."

He reached for her hand, but she shook her head. "I don't really dance."

"You don't *dance*?" He was waiting for the punch line.

"Not like that, I don't."

"Wait…you're actually serious, aren't you?" When she nodded, he couldn't stop himself from laughing, which earned him a withering look from Olivia.

"If I go onto the dance floor, people expect a lot out of me," she explained. "Like I'm supposed to be Ginger Rogers or something, even though my idea of a waltz is a lot different than theirs. It's embarrassing when I can't deliver what they expect. All dance training is *not* equal."

"I'll lead then."

Her eyebrows went up. Slightly suspicious and disbelieving, she asked, "*You* can dance?"

"Well enough not to step on your feet." He held out his hand again. She still looked suspicious. "Come on. What happened to trusting your partner?"

She cut her eyes at him, but didn't acknowledge that conversation otherwise. "You'd better not make me look bad," she warned, but she put her hand in his and let him lead her to the dance floor. Once there, he was able to pull her decently close to him in a special sort of torture. She smelled amazing and his hand found warm bare skin above the deep drape of her dress.

At first, Olivia was stiff in his arms, but after a few minutes, she relaxed a bit and followed his lead. It was nothing fancy—he stuck to the basic steps and she picked them up quickly—but Olivia was obviously impressed when she smiled at him. "You're good."

"You sound surprised."

"Because I am. I didn't peg you as the dancing type." The teasing smile took a little of the sting out of her words.

"Ah, well, I like women, and women *love* a man who'll take them dancing."

Olivia laughed. "That explains it, then. I knew there would be a good reason. So where'd you learn to dance like this?"

He led her through an easy turn and into a shallow dip. "The Recreational Dance Society of Jacksonville. Beginners always welcome."

"*Really?* In college?"

"Yes, really. Why the disbelief?"

She shook her head. "I just can't picture eighteen-year-old Evan Lawford taking time out of his partying to take dance lessons."

"Like I said, the ladies like it."

"I believe it, but you need a better story."

"Why?"

In all seriousness, she said, "Because the lady might not like to hear that you only dance in the ongoing quest to get into her panties."

He had to respect her blunt honesty. "Then what story should I tell?"

She really seemed to be thinking about it. "Um... Like your mom teaching you when you were little. Maybe dancing around the kitchen with your feet on hers. It's a sweet image and would work nicely."

He snorted at the idea and Olivia gave him an odd look. "There's no way I could say that with a straight face," he explained. "I come from a very conservative religious household. No dancing allowed."

"None?"

"No. Dancing inspires lust." He said it with snark, but his father *was* being proven partly right even as he spoke. Evan was certainly lusting after Olivia right now. Much more of this and he was going to have to loosen his hold to put more space between them before Olivia felt that lust.

To his surprise, she collapsed into giggles. "What's so funny?"

"You. Taking dance classes to rebel against your parents. That's got to be the strangest, yet most civilized form of rebellion I've ever heard of."

"Hey, there was plenty of other rebellion," he said in his own defense. "And long before college, thank you very much. There was just no place I could learn to dance in Arrowwood."

Her eyes narrowed suspiciously. "A whole *town* of people who don't dance? Did you grow up in that town in *Footloose* or something?"

"Yes, as a matter of fact, I did. Call me Kevin Bacon." When she continued to stare at him, waiting for his response, he finally shrugged and offered, "When your father is a hellfire preacher in the town's biggest church, no one is going to teach you to dance, even if you ask nicely."

Olivia was incredulous. "*You're* a *preacher's* kid? Oh. My. *God*." She started to laugh, but pressed her lips closed instead, making the sound come out as an unladylike snort. "That explains oh-so-much about you."

Damn it. He'd assumed she knew, but this proved that Jory had kept his promise and that information to himself. But the last thing he wanted was amateur psychology from Olivia. "Actually, that explains nothing about me."

"I beg to differ."

"Well, you'd be wrong." To throw her off-topic and off balance, he led her into a more complicated pattern that had her nearly tripping over her feet to catch up.

She shot him a dirty look, clearly aware of why he'd

done it. But "I thought you said no fancy moves," was all she said about it.

"Sorry. I thought you could handle it."

"You thought wrong. I still don't know what I'm doing."

There was a sigh in her voice that changed the subject nicely, even if she didn't mean for it to. But they'd been dancing—literally and figuratively—long enough.

He leaned close enough to drop his voice but still see her face. "Do you need a bit longer to feel me out, learn how my body moves and how we fit together?"

He felt her stiffen at the reminder of the words that had been haunting him, and she stumbled slightly again. She'd put the idea out there, though, so she had to have been expecting it to come back on her. A pink flush, evident even in the low light of the room, crawled up her chest to her neck. "I'm not sure we're quite in sync yet."

His thumb stroked the soft skin of her back, and he felt the muscle beneath jump in response. "I think we're getting there. You just need to let go and trust me to do my part."

That flush had made it to her cheeks, and he could see her pulse fluttering in the base of her throat. But when she lifted her eyes, they met his evenly. "That's the thing, Evan. I'm not sure I can."

And, that, sadly, was the truth. Even if Evan looked shocked to hear it.

She knew perfectly well what Evan was capable of—

and honestly, it only made it more difficult to make decisions. She had plenty of memories of exactly how they fit together, what his hands felt like and how he moved. And since he'd had nine years to improve on his technique, the possibilities made her knees a bit wobbly.

But knowing what he was capable of cut both ways, because she knew what he *wasn't* capable of, either. *That's* where she'd gotten burned before. And while she could talk a good game this time, she had to be honest with herself, too, and she wasn't completely sure she trusted herself to be okay with where that limit of capability was.

Evan was the scariest kind of womanizer: he genuinely liked women, and he could be caring and sweet—up to an extent. She didn't think it was an act he pulled just to lure women into his bed, because he didn't need to pretend anything to get women to accept a no-strings fling. The fact that easy, sexy charm probably *wasn't* an act was what made him so dangerous. Even knowing what she knew, even after he'd hurt her before, even telling herself exactly where the line would be going in…it still didn't bode well for her in the end.

And she'd be a fool to set herself up for the hurt—however unintentional—this could cause.

"You can't what? Let go? Or trust me?" Evan asked. There was tight humor in his voice—he didn't seem angry or hurt, just curious, surprised and maybe, just *maybe*, a touch offended.

The song changed, and Evan altered his pace, but not the steps—which they'd now repeated enough that she didn't have to think too much about her feet. But it did remind her that they were not alone: a couple hundred of Miami's wealthy and elite surrounded them. "This isn't an appropriate place for this conversation, Evan."

It was a viable, reasonable excuse—and she'd jumped on it for exactly that reason.

"There's loud music and lots of booze. No one's paying any attention to us, sweetheart."

Okay, different tack. She might as well be up-front and honest. "I thought we were going to be friends."

"We are. Look at us. Perfectly friendly."

"Then why are you making a pass at me? I thought you said you'd respect my wishes."

"I said I'd respect it if you said 'no.' I didn't say I wouldn't ask." He pulled her a little closer and the effect was devastating. "And you haven't said 'no,' yet."

And that was a glaring and very telling lack of action on her part. While Evan might be lots of less-than-gentlemanly-things, she didn't doubt he would back down as soon as she said it. Yet somehow the magic word wouldn't make it past her lips. She was a fool, but she'd put herself in this position willingly, knowing she'd have to make the choice sooner or later.

She had weaknesses—plenty of them—and she always had to balance the want against the price she might later pay for the indulgence. Everything was a trade-off: she might have a slice of chocolate cake, but skip the bread, or she'd do extra sit-ups the next day to work off some of the extra calories. As long as she didn't eat cake every night, it wasn't a problem.

Everything in moderation. Splurge occasionally because life was short. You only live once.

Evan was a splurge. And far more tempting than any chocolate cake. The big question, though, was could she enjoy Evan in moderation this time?

Evan hadn't said a word the whole time she went over things in her mind. He'd just kept dancing, kept stroking his thumb over her back and raising goose bumps on her skin, waiting for her to answer.

She took a deep breath and met his eyes. The heat there should have scorched her. "I haven't said no, but then, you haven't actually asked me a question, either."

Evan finally stopped moving. The hand he was still holding shifted slightly, keeping them palm to palm but allowing his fingers to thread through hers and squeeze gently. "Do you want to get out of here?"

Moment of truth time.

She only hesitated for a second.

"Yes."

Evan seemed genuinely surprised at her answer, and for a split second, Olivia wondered if he'd just been messing with her, teasing her and flirting without expectation.

Because if so…well, she'd have to kill him.

But then she noticed the way his fingers continued to tighten around hers and the slow, sexy smile. "Good."

Their exit was hurried and as sly as possible. Evan mumbled something about not wanting to make the entire rounds and Olivia agreed. She grabbed her wrap and purse and tried to look dignified—just in case—as they slipped out the door and into the stairwell headed to the parking deck.

Her heels clacked on the metal stairs and it echoed in the emptiness. Evan kept a hand on her elbow to steady her down the first two flights, but on the next landing, he stopped, trapping her between his body and the wall and causing her heartbeat to kick into double time.

Then his hand was cupping her cheek and tilting her head to his and…

Sweet mercy. This was probably a big mistake. A decision she was going to regret.

But the regret would come later, and right now, she had this. Her purse dropped to the floor, forgotten, as she gripped the lapels of his jacket.

Evan's kiss was everything she remembered and more. Unhurried but hungry, it promised all kinds of pleasures to come, and pure *want* drowned out any cautions from her higher brain functions.

He tasted like the whiskey on the rocks he'd been drinking earlier, only hot and far more potent. Then he leaned into her, pressing her back against the cool cinder block wall, deepening the kiss and blocking out everything that wasn't him.

And his hands…one was gentle against her cheek, but the other was strong against her hip—both of them caressing and stoking the fire kindled by his tongue.

She slid her hands under his jacket to feel the hard muscles of his stomach hidden under fine cotton, then wrapped her arms around his waist to pull him against her.

A groan echoed off the walls, and she wasn't sure

if it was hers or his. Evan's lips were hot against her neck, sending shivers over her skin. Hooking a foot around his calf, she pulled his thigh between hers and squeezed, trying to release some of the tension building inside her.

"Liv." Evan mumbled against her neck as a tremor rocked his body against hers. The hand that had been kneading her hip reached for hers as he pressed another hard kiss against her lips, then he bent down to get her purse and pushed through the door into the parking deck.

Olivia followed on shaky legs. At the car, Evan stopped to kiss her again, and she nearly climbed him like a tree, wanting more. Whispering a promise that made her blush, Evan opened her door. She scrambled inside as Evan went to the driver's side.

Some of her hair had come down—or been pulled down by Evan's hands—and she could feel the French twist now wobbling drunkenly on her head. Not caring or bothering with a mirror, she searched for the other pins and let it all fall loose around her shoulders with a big shake. Evan paused as he put the car in gear to run his hands through the messy curls, then used it to tug her over to his side for another kiss. "I don't know how I'm going to get us home."

"Drive fast."

Evan grinned at the command, and tires squealed as he accelerated. They were both quiet, and Olivia wondered if the pounding of her heart was audible to Evan as his hand landed on her knee and moved up to gently stroke the sensitive skin of her inner thigh. Her nails dug into the leather seat as the muscles began to quiver. She let her head fall back against the headrest and closed her eyes as his fingers moved slowly, maddeningly, *dangerously* higher.

But was it actually dangerous? A little voice inside her was shouting a warning, but it was easy enough to ignore. Dumping old emotions on top of this would be a mistake. She was an adult, not some starry-eyed kid, and *this* was not the same as last time at all.

Evan was hot and sexy and occasionally sweet, and there were far worse reasons to have sex. There was no reason to overthink this. Evan's fingers moved another crucial inch. Hell, why was she even thinking at all when she could just *feel*?

Mercy.

All that attention to *feeling* meant Olivia had no idea how long she'd been in the car or even where they were, but Evan was killing the engine and coming around to open her door. The breeze and the play of the lights told her they were near water, but she had no idea *which* water and she lacked enough knowledge of Miami as a whole to even hazard a guess.

Wherever they were, it was gorgeously landscaped and lush—the building not brand-new, but not shabby either, and the fact it wasn't a high-rise meant they might be off one of the canals, but not right off the bay. She had no idea. But, really, it didn't matter. Evan paused long enough to give her another kiss before leading her up the path to his door.

She half expected Evan to grab her, sweep her off her feet and carry her to the bedroom the second the door closed behind them, but instead, she found herself pulled gently into a long, unhurried kiss. He took her purse and wrap and laid them on a table before tossing his keys on top and shrugging out of his suit coat. She took a deep breath as an anticipatory shiver ran over her.

"Can I get you a drink or something?" he asked as he loosened his tie.

The air rushed out of her lungs. *Was he kidding?* She was so primed that one more touch might do the trick and Evan was playing Gracious Host? Hell, the only thing keeping her from dragging *him* to the bedroom was the fact she didn't know where the bedroom *was*.

"I'm good, thanks," she lied. More accurately, she felt like an idiot, standing in his foyer like an unsuspecting prom date who'd just been friendzoned.

"You sure? Wine? Water?"

"I'm *sure*." She didn't like the tone of her voice, but it couldn't be helped.

In a snap, the Gracious Host was gone, replaced by an almost predatory look that weakened her knees. "Good. That way," he pointed.

"Finally," she said honestly, slipping out of her shoes and following him. "I thought we were about to have a tea party."

"Hey, I was just trying to be nice."

"Noted. Appreciated."

Evan backed into a room, pulling her with him, and she could see the bed just over his shoulder.

"But I didn't come here for nice," she added.

A split second later, she was flat on her back on that bed with Evan looming over her. "Since you put it that way…"

She wasn't sure if that was a warning or a promise, but she was okay either way. Evan straddled her hips, his eyes watching hers as he unbuttoned his shirt and tossed it aside.

Oh yes. Very nice. It might be shallow, but Olivia spent every day in the company of men who, by the nature of their careers, had excellent bodies. *That* set a standard difficult for an average guy to meet. But Evan…oh, he'd do *nicely.* Plenty of definition and strength on display without being overly brawny or muscle-bound. A light sprinkling of hair accented his pecs before narrowing to a trail that bisected a nice set of abs and disappeared into the waistband of his pants. Her fingers itched to trace that line, and she did, following it from his belt buckle to his sternum, loving the way the muscles contracted under her touch.

Evan tugged her dress up over her hips, nearly to her ribs, before pulling her up to slide it up and off. Olivia had that one moment of self-consciousness but tried to push it aside. Evan had seen her naked before; he knew what he was getting. She had no breasts to speak of, no "womanly" curves. She was just as far from the lingerie model ideal figure as any other woman. It was a double standard, she knew, to expect a certain physique from a man while she offered a bony, boobless body in return, but Evan didn't seem to mind any more now than he had then.

If anything, Evan seemed to like it, his eyes hooded and dark as his hands mapped a path for his lips to follow. Her breasts might be small, but they were very sensitive, and the rasp of his tongue over her nipple had her arching off the bed, begging for more.

She'd been a virgin the first time with Evan, too naive to not confuse love and sex, and too nervous to fully appreciate the experience. But tonight…*mercy*.

Her hands were shaking with need, making her attempts at his belt and zipper clumsy. Evan finally took over, shucking his clothes and giving her the skin to skin contact she craved. His skin was hot, his body heavy on hers, his fingers and tongue working black magic on her until she wanted to scream.

So she did.

Olivia's thighs squeezed him like a vise, threatening to crack a rib as she came against his mouth. Evan felt the shock wave roll through her body and redoubled his efforts, working his tongue until she was tugging at his hair, pulling him up and over her and wrapping those long powerful legs around his hips.

The sight of Olivia nearly stopped his heart. That golden-red hair was wild and tangled, and her skin was flushed pink and glistened under a sheen of sweat. She opened her eyes, dark with desire but focused directly on his, and used those legs to leverage him closer.

He knelt between her thighs, indulging his need to

touch her. Her skin was so soft, but it draped over steel-hard muscle that fluttered as his fingers touched it. He'd seen her in action; he knew she was strong and had seen what she could do with her body, and it gave him a primal level of satisfaction to see her body react so strongly because of him.

But that strength put him in a tug-of-war—her pulling him closer, him holding back, wanting to touch and explore with leisure—that he wasn't entirely sure he'd be able to win, even if he really wanted to.

He anchored himself and slid his hands over her ribs to her breasts, tracing light circles around her nipples. Olivia's eyes rolled back in her head and teeth caught her bottom lip.

"Ev-*an*…"

The breathy, exasperated plea made him smile. He squeezed a nipple gently, causing her to groan. "Yes, Liv?"

Her hand grabbed his wrist. "Don't tease."

"But you said not to rush the foreplay, remember?"

"You're evil." A tiny tremor shook her body and she released his wrist. "And you're killing me."

He wanted to feel smug, but Liv's hand had slithered down between them, palming him and working him with gentle, insistent pressure that threatened to snap his control. His hands were shaking as he reached for the nightstand drawer and grabbed a condom. "I know the feeling."

That earned him a smile that turned wicked as she took the condom from him, turning a simple, usually perfunctory action into an erotic one that left him groaning and wheezing for air.

"Now who's teas—?" The question was cut short as Olivia lifted her hips and guided him in.

He lost the ability to speak—the ability to even *think*—as all his higher brain functions shut down, narrowing his focus to one thing, and Olivia's deeply satisfied sigh echoed his own.

He moved slowly at first, taking his time, loving the way Olivia responded—earnestly, wholeheartedly and enthusiastically—the little moans spurring him on. He wanted to savor, prolong it, but he'd been waiting for nine years to have Olivia in his bed again, and that re-solve was weakening under the need to lose himself in her completely.

She was thrashing, fisting the sheets and moving her hips frantically, trying to increase the pace. Roll-ing to his back, he pulled Olivia atop him to let her take the lead.

Her hair fell like a curtain around them, blocking out everything else as she rocked against him, finding her groove and driving him insane. When her eyes glazed over and her rhythm faltered, he grabbed her hips and took over, slamming into her again and again until she arched nearly in half, her whole body shuddering and shivering as her orgasm moved through her.

It was beautiful to watch, but her climax pushed him over the edge, causing him to explode with enough force to make his vision go fuzzy at the edges.

When he was finally able to think again, Olivia was

draped over his chest, her breath still heaving. Carefully, he pushed her hair out of his face and hers, gathering it into a loose ponytail and wrapping it around his fist.

Olivia smiled, but her eyes stayed closed. "Thanks. It was bothering me but I couldn't be bothered to find the energy to move it."

"Well, that was about all the energy I had left. I may be dead now."

Her fingers stroked slowly over his chest, then she opened her eyes. "Pity."

Amazingly, that was enough to stir his blood, if no other part of his body. "Just give me a minute or two."

"Yay." After a heavy sigh, she asked, "Am I too heavy? Do I need to move?"

The woman weighed nothing, and she felt amazing anyway. "No."

"Good." After another sigh, she seemed to doze off.

Since the only remaining option was for him to lie here and think—which he really didn't want to do— he did the same.

CHAPTER SIX

OLIVIA EASING OUT of bed woke him up. Sunshine streamed in through curtains he'd forgotten to close, telling him they'd slept pretty late.

But then they hadn't gotten much sleep before the sun came up, either. He felt wrung-out and sore in muscles he didn't know he had, but the deep, sated satisfaction well made up for that.

Olivia stretched, bending herself into another of those impossible positions. It was kind of sexy, until he heard a sharp crack.

"Ouch."

She started, then looked over her shoulder. "Just wait," she said with a weak smile and proceeded to crack seemingly each and every joint in her body—including some he didn't know *could* crack. "Ah, that's better."

"Good lord, Olivia. It sounds like you're falling apart."

She shrugged. "I'm in pretty good shape for my age, so I'm lucky."

She was in excellent—amazing—shape. "For your *age*?"

"Sadly, I can't be twenty-one forever. A couple of my friends have already retired, but they had injuries that tipped the scale a little early. If I make it to thirty-five, I'll be happy." She reached for the shirt he'd thrown on the floor last night and slipped into it. "I need water. I'm as dry as the Sahara this morning. Do you want anything?" she called as she disappeared down the hallway.

He grabbed a pair of boxers and followed her. "I'll make coffee."

"Oh, that will be excellent. But water first." She poured a full glass and drank deeply as he filled the pot and measured coffee. The initial morning-after awkwardness that they avoided by Olivia's snap-crackle-pop routine settled in belatedly and they stood there silently as the coffee brewed.

Finally, he asked, "Do you need to be home at a specific time today?"

"Not really. I've got some sewing and laundry to do, but I have Sundays off unless we're performing or something. But," she quickly added, setting down her glass, "I don't want to keep you from whatever you need to do today. I can call a cab or…"

"I've got no plans." He paused and reached for the hem of the shirt she wore, tugging her a few inches closer. "Yet."

"Well, all I have is the dress I wore last night. It rather limits my options."

"You don't need clothes for what I'm planning."

"I'm intrigued."

"Good."

Olivia was angling in for a kiss when a loud, fast guitar riff played and her purse began vibrating against the table. She pulled back as if she'd been burned.

"It's okay," he said, "You can answer it."

"I'd really rather not."

In that second he recognized the tune and realized why it was familiar. At that point, he wanted to put even more space between them. There was really only one person Olivia would assign that particular song to on her phone because it was one of his favorite songs: Jory.

He didn't know why she might not feel like talking to her brother at the moment, but it served him up a heaping load of guilt for his behavior. Not for sleeping with Olivia—he had no regrets—but because he knew he *should* feel bad for not staying away from Jory's sister. It was a fine hair to split—but one he'd been splitting all his life. He might be sorry what he did was a sin, but only *because* it was a sin. But he wouldn't be sorry he did it because he'd enjoyed it and would do it again if the opportunity presented itself. His father, needless to say, hadn't been pleased with that bit of amateur theology runaround. Where he and Olivia were concerned, he doubted Jory would be impressed with that logic either, and forgiveness wouldn't be easily given.

"That's Jory's ringtone," Olivia explained unnecessarily, then she shook her head. "Maybe I shouldn't have brought him up right now. You know, all things considered."

"Well, one of us had to."

"But my brother and my sex life aren't really something I like to discuss in the same conversation."

"I'm sure Jory feels the same way. But," he added, "You and me? It's kind of hard *not* to bring him in."

"Ew. Gross."

"Liv," he chided, "You know what I mean."

"I do. I also know that I'm an adult and it's none of my brother's business who I sleep with."

"True."

Olivia looked uncomfortable. "How much does Jory know? About before, I mean."

"You don't know?"

"I know he knows something, but he certainly doesn't talk about it, and he wasn't keen on even the *idea* of us hooking up." She shrugged. "But you two are friends."

Evan had no idea where to go from there. "Does it matter? That's ancient history."

"Except that it's news now, isn't it?"

"Is it?"

Olivia sighed. "Look, I'll be honest with you if you'll be honest with me."

That was almost ominous. "Seems fair," he said carefully.

"Honestly, the less Jory knows about my sex life the better. And as I said, it's none of his business who I sleep with."

"I happen to agree with you on that."

"So, I don't see the need to tell Jory about this. Do you?"

"I can assure you that your brother does not want me anywhere near you, so no, I don't see the need to tell him anything either."

Instead of agreement, he got a surprised look from her. "Why is that?"

"Because as you said, it's none of Jory's business."

"No. Why do you say Jory doesn't want you near me?"

"Because you're his sister." Surely she understood that.

"But you're his friend. If you're good enough for him to hang out with, why aren't you good enough for me?"

Oh, where to begin. "Because."

"Because?"

He poured coffee, stalling, and when that didn't work, he tried to shrug it off. "Yeah, because."

"Is this some kind of weird guy thing?"

"Yes," he said, hoping she'd leave it at that. "It's a guy thing."

"How juvenile. It's like you're still teenagers."

He was beginning to agree. Hell, hadn't he already convinced himself there was a big difference between an eighteen-year-old sister and a twenty-seven-year-old sister? But that might just be wishful thinking on his part.

"So sisters are completely off-limits?" she asked

and waited until he nodded. "That's insane. What if we were to fall in love?"

Evan spit his coffee across the counter, burning his lip in the process. "Whoa, there. Liv, I—um…"

She waved a hand and passed him a towel. "Oh, calm down. It's purely a rhetorical question. It just seems unfair. Does he get to put other, nonrelated women off-limits?"

"No."

"Then that's just ridiculous. Either it's his business who you sleep with or it isn't."

"It's more complicated than that."

"Only because boys are weird."

"Oh, and girls aren't? One of your girlfriends would be okay if you slept with her brother?"

That gave her a second's pause. "I wouldn't know. Unless that girl's brother was also dancing in the same company, the chances of me meeting him are slim. Anyway, dancers are a small community. Chances are whoever you're sleeping with has slept with someone else you know anyway. The grown-up thing to do is to butt the hell out of any sex that doesn't currently involve you."

She had a refreshing, mature approach that didn't help at all in this instance. "I'd agree, but the last time I slept with you, Jory practically broke my nose. Right, wrong or indifferent, Jory *does* have strong opinions when it comes to me and you."

Olivia blinked. "He did *what*?"

He cursed. "Nothing. You want some breakfast?"

"Oh, no, you can't drop something like that and just move on. So Jory does know we hooked up?"

He could lie. It only depended on which Madison sibling he wanted to anger today. From the look on Olivia's face, it was probably safer for him to tell the truth to her. "Yes."

"And he was mad about it."

"Yes."

"Why? And don't give me any 'because of a Guy Thing' crap."

"Aside from the 'Guy Thing crap'—which is not crap, by the way—you don't screw around—literally or not—with someone's sister when you have nothing to offer."

"Every woman is someone's sister."

"Then let me rephrase—"

"No need," she interrupted. "It'll never make sense. But if Jory was so mad about this, how come he never said anything to me about it?"

"Because once it was over and done with, there was no need." He could hope she'd accept that at face value.

"That little…" She shook her head slowly. "I'm going to kill him."

"Olivia…"

"Don't," she warned. "Jory told you to back off, didn't he?" She didn't wait for his answer. "*That's* why you dumped me like that."

"In all fairness, you were leaving for London—"

"New York," she corrected.

"—or wherever in another couple of weeks or so. What difference did it make?"

"It made a hell of a difference to me. *Jory* makes a decision, *I* get dumped and *you* get to be the bad guy. He comes out smelling like a rose. I'm going to *kill* him."

"Liv, be serious. You're getting all worked up over something that happened years ago. And Jory really did mean well."

"Oh, as long as he *meant* well, that changes everything," she snarked. "I'll just forget all the hurt and shame and stuff since he 'meant well'."

Somehow he was the rational person in the conversation. Jory owed him big-time. "How would you going off to New York feeling like you had some kind of attachment to me have been at all good for your career?"

"I wasn't 'attached' to you," she mumbled.

"Really? Then why did it hurt?" Her lips flattened and she looked deep into her coffee cup. His point made, he continued. "But that way, you went off, with nothing holding you back. And being mad at me was far preferable to you being mad at Jory, right?"

"Why are you being so damn reasonable about this?"

"Because I happen to think Jory was right." It had been the right thing—for everyone.

That took some of the wind out of her sails. "Wow. You really are a cold, heartless bastard."

"So you've said."

She lifted her chin. "So what about last night, then?"

"There's a big difference between then and now. Not

only are you an adult, you're established in your career and your life—there's not much for me to screw up for you now. I've been very honest about what I wanted, so if you did make that choice, my conscience could be clear."

Olivia rubbed her temples. "I'm not sure how to process this."

"Then or now?"

"Either. Both. It's going to take a little time for me to make sense of it." She looked at him. "Here's the thing about now, though—*I'm* not worried about Jory or what he thinks. Are you?"

There was a clear challenge there that was impossible to fully answer. "I brought you home last night, remember? But, no, I don't see the need to rub Jory's nose in it. I may not be the best of friends, but I hope I'm better than that."

"If it makes you feel better," she said quietly, the quick change of mood surprising him, "I think you're a really good friend to Jory."

He certainly didn't feel like it. "Yes, because sleeping with his baby sister is the true sign of friendship."

"But you don't want him to be upset, so that says something. Does it make me a bad sister to sleep with my brother's best friend?"

"Well, when you put it like that…"

"The thing is, I can see where the idea of possibly being put in the middle or forced to choose sides comes into this, but that's an issue *any* time two people you know—especially if you know them independently of each other—are involved. It's selfish to demand other people adjust *their* behavior so that *you* aren't made uncomfortable at some point. And it's insane to think you *could* put those demands on people. It's like telling a married couple they can't get divorced because it will mess up the seating charts at your future dinner parties." He started to argue, but Olivia lifted a hand to stop him. "I don't like to think about my brother having sex, either, so you know what I do? *I don't think about it.*"

He couldn't help but laugh. "That's very logical, Olivia."

"Thank you."

"But people, as a whole, aren't logical. Especially about people they love. Or sex."

"Then it's your call. I'll leave now, if that's what you want."

"I didn't say that. But Jory won't forgive me if you get hurt again."

"Your ego is simply astounding." She shook her head.

"It has nothing to do with ego."

She sighed, then shrugged. "Well, if you don't think you can handle me, that's fine." She set her coffee cup on the counter. "I'll go get dressed. Call me a cab, will you?" she called over her shoulder as she headed back down the hall.

He caught her in the bedroom and tackled her to the bed. "Can I handle you? Liv, honey, I thought I proved that last night. *Repeatedly.* The real question is…can you handle me?"

"I think that was proven last night, as well."

He pretended to think as he worked the buttons of her shirt open. "Maybe we should try it one more time. Just to be sure."

"Might take more than *one* more time," she said. "You know, to be *absolutely* sure."

His conscience sent up a small protest, but Olivia was sliding out of that shirt and…

Well, at least he could say he tried.

There was nothing quite like orgasms to completely change a girl's outlook on life.

It was rather silly, actually, as nothing else in her life had changed at all, but Olivia had to admit she was in a much better mood. Like a pressure valve had been opened.

Endorphins, she thought. *Amazing things.*

There was a slight soreness to muscles that hadn't been used like that in a long while, but the little frizzle of energy remaining in her blood was well worth the trade-off. And while Evan had brought her home early last night, the sheer amount of energy expended on what would normally be her lazy day off left her feeling a little tired and hungover as she warmed up at the barre Monday morning.

But even with that, she still felt it was worth it. No regrets at all.

She wasn't sure she could say the same about Evan,

though. She had to respect the level of loyalty to Jory that would make a player like Evan think twice about sleeping with a woman, but it dinged her pride as well—as if she had to talk him into it or something. Her inner femme fatale was a little miffed.

But everyone kept asking her about the smirk on her face, so she couldn't be *too* miffed about it. Or stay that way for very long. After all, once Evan had gotten past the whole Jory's-sister thing, she could make no complaints about his performance.

She even felt a bit better about the way Evan had treated her before. It still stung, and she still needed to kill Jory, but she had to look at it in a different light now. If nothing else, it made it a little easier to reconcile her attraction to Evan *now*. At least she didn't have to feel completely shallow or masochistic about it anymore.

As for what would happen next…possibly the best part of this was that she didn't *need* to worry about "next"—no matter what it might be. There was a very nice freedom in that.

"Earth to Olivia?" Theo waved a hand in front of her face. "Can you move so we can put the barres away?"

She'd spaced out, moving through the warm-up by rote and habit, and now she was busted. "Sorry," she muttered and went to stretch, figuring she'd use the time to get her head back in the studio where it belonged before she hurt herself.

Theo followed her. "You okay?"

"Yeah." She put her foot on the barre and lay over

her leg. "Just a little out of it today," she offered as an explanation.

"Career, money or sex?"

"Excuse me?" she asked.

"It's got to be one of the three. The smirk on your face means it's probably good, so that strikes worries about family and health off the list of topics to space out over."

"I'm putting my money on sex." Tina, one of younger soloists, propped her foot up onto the barre next to them.

"Oh, really?" Theo asked eagerly, totally ignoring the shut-up-please look Olivia shot him. "And why is that?"

"Leslie, that new apprentice—"

"Which one is she?" he interrupted.

"Kinda short, dark hair. Bad feet but pretty turns?"

Nodding, he said, "Okay, go on."

"Leslie works for a catering company that did the big Abrams Corporation party Saturday night and Olivia was there. With a very good-looking guy, too."

Olivia hadn't seen anyone she knew, but then there'd been a lot of people there, and she hadn't been paying all that much attention to the staff. *Damn.*

"How interesting."

"I know. Leslie didn't recognize the guy, though. Then she got busy and forgot to ask."

Good lord. They were gossiping about her as though she wasn't even there. She stood up. "*Ahem.*"

"Shh," Theo said, pushing her back down over her leg. "You stretch." He turned back to Tina. "*And...?*"

"*And* Olivia left early with Mr. Tall, Hot and Anonymous."

"So definitely sex, then. Okay, 'fess up, Olivia," he said, tapping her on the back. "Who is he?"

She didn't even bother to lift her head. "Oh, so *now* I get to be a part of this conversation?"

"Yes, please. We want details."

"The juicy ones," Tina added.

She didn't want to be the subject of dressing room gossip, and demurring to answer all but guaranteed she would be. But that did not mean she was willing to confirm speculations about her sex life for the company to further discuss at their leisure. "He's my brother's college roommate."

"Oh." Tina looked disappointed, and Olivia bit back a smile. While the truth of that statement might be causing *her*—and Evan—problems, she had to love it a little, too. A complete, concise, easy-peasy speculation shut down without any of the "he's just a friend" vague denials that would be met with even *more* probing. "But if he's hot *and* important enough to get an invite to the Abrams's do, give him my number."

Hell, she wasn't sure she had Tina's number even if she did want to offer Evan up like that. "I'll let him know you're available."

"Please do," Tina said and went back to the other side of the room, presumably to tell the others what new info she had.

She smacked him, hard. "Gee, thanks, Theo."

"What?" he said, rubbing his arm.

"Did you really *have* to encourage her? She's still annoyed that I got 'her' contract. Way to give her more ammo against me."

"That contract was only Tina's in her dreams. She's lucky her big butt ever made it out of the corps." He waved it off. "So are you going to tell me about this guy or not?"

"I need to go change my shoes."

"Come on."

She sighed. "I already told you. He's my brother's college roommate. He needed a date for the party, and I had nothing better to do. So I went. And I met Matt Abrams, so that's not too shabby, either."

"And your smug mood today is caused by…?"

"I had a good time." She wasn't going to offer more than that, and Theo could infer anything he liked from it. She trusted Theo not to provide grist for the rumor mill. Of course, it helped that she had some dirt on him, and he knew it.

After a moment, Theo nodded. "Good for you, sweetie. Now, I'll let you go change your shoes, as I'm pretty sure Sylvie is going to want to run through the *adage* first."

Olivia took a second to check her phone while she was at it and found a text from Evan: You busy tonight?

It made her smile and put a sizzle in her blood at the same time she gave it a mental side-eye. There was a definite overtone of booty call to the message, which part of her felt she *should* be offended by. At the same time, the memories of yesterday were fresh enough to make her glad of an encore.

Theo was calling for her, forcing her to make a decision. I'll be done by 5:30, she typed quickly and dropped the phone back into her bag. There was no sense second-guessing herself, and there was no reason not to enjoy herself while she could.

With the decision made and the rationale accepted, she found her mind much clearer and her usual concentration returned. In fact, she almost forgot about Evan all together until later that afternoon when Leslie-the-apprentice mentioned seeing her at the party. That sent her back to her phone during the water break to see if he'd responded.

I'll pick you up at your place on my way home. 6:30-ish.

The rest of the afternoon dragged by.

Broiled chicken and steamed veggies. It wasn't exciting, but Olivia was forcing him to eat better these days. Well, not *forcing*—she actually hadn't said anything about his diet—but a man could only eat junk while his dinner partner ate healthy so many times before guilt set in. He'd buckled under in less than a week. Olivia still hadn't said anything, but she'd smirked when he told her tonight's menu.

"It's ready," he called, setting the plates on the coffee table. Olivia came out of the bedroom in yoga pants and a tank top, braiding her hair as she walked.

"Good, I'm starved. Thank you for cooking."

As she settled beside him, he noticed her bright pink socks. "Are you cold?"

She paused, a forkful of chicken partway to her mouth. "No. Why?" He indicated the socks and she shrugged. "Oh, that. I've just got ugly feet."

He honestly hadn't paid that much attention to her feet before—he'd been too busy focusing on other, more interesting parts of her anatomy. "They can't be that bad."

"Oh, yeah they can. This is yummy, by the way."

He'd seen pointe shoes. There was no way they didn't do bad things to her feet. "Let me see them."

She crossed her legs, tucking her feet under her thighs. "No way."

"Come on," he cajoled. She shook her head and took a bite. "I'm going to see them eventually."

"Maybe. But not now. It'll kill your appetite."

"One of my first jobs in college was at a restaurant. I cooked, washed dishes, scrubbed the grills. It tore my hands up."

"My parents own a restaurant. I'm well aware of what it does to your hands."

He put his fork down. "Well, my first college girl-friend dumped me because she said my hands were troll-like, and she didn't like them touching her."

"What a witch."

"True, but my point is, I understand."

"Look, even *I* think my feet are gross. I'm not show-

ing them off. *No*," she added when he started to protest. "End of subject."

"It's not like I can't sneak a peek later."

"That's up to you. I can warn you, but I can't stop
you." She shook her head. "You might regret it, though."

"You've got some weird hang-ups," he mumbled.

She smiled at him angelically. "Everyone's crazy in
their own special way. The trick is to find the person
who thinks your special brand of crazy is kinda cute."

"You've got a special brand there, that's for sure,"
he mumbled toward his chicken.

"Where did you work?"

He let her change the subject, since she obviously
felt strongly about it. "The Carousel."

"That place on the beach where the waitresses wear
bikinis?"

"That's the one. How do you know about The Carousel?"

"Who in Florida *doesn't* know about that place?
It's legendary. I never got to go, of course, but I've
heard stories from friends and other people who went
to Jacksonville for spring break." She shook her head.
"Wow. When you decided to rebel against your up-
bringing, you went all out, didn't you? Dancing, drinking, women, working in a place like that. Were you
trying to mark off all seven deadly sins or just break
half the Ten Commandments?"

"I had a punch card. Every tenth sin earned me a free
ice cream cone to enjoy in my front row seat in hell."

"So much for a 'civilized' rebellion."

"It takes more than a few dance lessons to really rebel."

"What did your parents think?"

"I didn't tell them anything, but this girl from high school was also going to school in Jacksonville and come summer break, she went home and told *everyone* all my sins."

She shook her head in sympathy. "I hate people like that."

"Me, too. My father threatened to disown me, my mother cried because they were so embarrassed I'd turned my back on everything they'd tried to teach me. Big drama."

"But look at you now. You're certainly doing well for yourself. They can't be too upset with how you turned out."

He shrugged.

"They're not? Why?"

"Honestly, I have no idea if they are or not. I don't even know if they know how I turned out. I haven't been back to Arrowwood since the day I left, and I haven't spoken to my parents in ten, maybe eleven, years."

"I'm so sorry."

Of course Olivia would think that a tragedy. She had great parents. "I'm not. It's better this way. Everyone's much happier, I promise."

Carefully, she asked, "So there's no chance for reconciliation?"

He leaned back and studied her. "Show me your feet."

"What?"

"If you want to talk about my parents, you have to show me your feet. It's only fair if we *both* do something we don't want to."

She actually seemed to consider it. "Point taken. I won't pry anymore. But I *am* sorry you have unreasonable and judgmental parents."

"Thanks, Liv. Now you know why I've always preferred yours." That reminded him, especially since Olivia hadn't mentioned it yet. "Speaking of your parents, have you talked to them today?"

She shook her head. "Mom called earlier but I was in rehearsals. She left a message for me to call tomorrow. Wait—why do you ask?"

"I normally go to your parents' for Thanksgiving, you know."

Olivia looked at her plate. "I'd forgotten about that."

"Dee called today and asked me to give you a lift to Tampa."

"You're kidding."

"You don't have a car, Olivia. It makes sense."

"But I've lined up a rental. I *want* to drive."

"They're just worried about you driving Alligator Alley on your own at night."

"I'm an adult. I've been on my own for years. I've navigated foreign cities where no one speaks English. I think I can handle a four-hour drive through central Florida all by myself."

"But the cell reception sucks through there. I see their point, even if you are too skinny for the alligators to bother eating."

She shot him a sour look for that crack. "I'm going up on Wednesday, but I have to come back Friday night. I'm in the Santa parade on Saturday. You shouldn't have to cut your holiday short because of me."

"I've got plans on Saturday myself. It works out fine."

Olivia muttered under her breath.

"Give in graciously to make your parents happy, and I promise I won't look at your feet when you're naked later," he offered as a compromise.

"But I *wanted* to drive. I haven't driven since August."

"Fine. I'll let you drive part of the way. Will that make you happy?"

She grinned. "Oh, I was hoping you'd say that. Deal. I can leave anytime after four on Wednesday."

CHAPTER SEVEN

It took them longer than expected to get to Tampa. They blamed it on traffic, and everyone accepted that explanation without question. Thankfully, no one seemed to notice they were a bit more rumpled than they should be after the drive.

Evan, though, felt a little bad about the delay when he dropped Olivia at the Madisons' and saw the genuine excitement and misty eyes of Olivia's homecoming. They were truly an ideal family, straight out of a greeting card commercial—Dee fussing when she found out they hadn't eaten yet, and Gary offering him gas money for the trip. He declined both the money and the offer of food and left for Jory's place. Olivia thanked him for the ride politely and with the right amount of distance, but she had a small, I've-got-a-secret smile on her face as he left.

He got another helping of guilt when he got to Jory's twenty minutes later. He'd delayed seeing his best friend in order to see his best friend's sister naked—which he wasn't about to admit. He tossed his gear into Jory's "guest room"—which was more of a weight room with a twin bed from Jory's childhood bedroom tucked in the corner—while Jory got them both beers.

Like his sister, Jory chose to live downtown, doing his part to help gentrify an area trying to reinvent itself. It was a stark contrast to his parents' suburban lifestyle, but Jory had taken to it perfectly, all the way down to the local microbrewed beer he offered. A perfect example of a young, upwardly mobile lawyer with a hipster bent.

They caught up on a few things, then Jory said, "By the way, thanks for driving Livvy up."

"Not a problem."

"I told Mom not to ask you, but she still worries about Olivia."

"I was coming this way anyway, so it made sense."

"And it went all right?" Jory asked carefully.

That was probably as close as Jory was going to come to bringing up Evan's past with Olivia. He hadn't mentioned it since the day Evan had agreed to leave Liv alone. "It was fine. It's been a long time—too long for old grudges."

Jory snorted. "You obviously don't know my sister very well. She can carry a grudge with the best of them."

He'd say he was getting to know Olivia pretty well these days. And while Olivia could carry a grudge, she seemed equally capable of letting it go. But there was really no way to offer that information to Jory. "She didn't bring it up today, so I didn't either. I'm pretty sure she's over it." That wasn't a lie. They'd talked the whole way up, but not about that. "By the way, I brought wine for tomorrow," he said to change the subject. "Don't let me forget it."

Jory nodded. "Livvy didn't need that kind of baggage back then. She'd have gotten far more attached to you than you to her, and it would have ended badly. Who knows how that could have thrown her off, and she was just starting out. A clean break was the only way for her."

"In retrospect, I agree with you."

"I appreciate that. And, seriously, I wanted my sister to like you—and you her—just not like that." He laughed. Evan tried, but he was having a hard time seeing the humor. "I'm not counting on you two being friends, but it'd be nice to know you could at least stand each other. We'd all feel better knowing there's someone close by she could call if she were ever in a pinch."

So Jory's ban on Evan and Olivia contact wasn't complete. Just with the assumption they'd remain vertical and clothed. Evan bit back a smile—at least once, they had. It'd been quick, but far hotter than anticipated. "She has my contact info, and I've told her not to hesitate to call if she needs anything."

"Good. And thanks. Did she happen to mention anything about a boyfriend to you?"

Evan nearly choked on his beer. "No. Why?"

"Livvy's been hard to get in touch with lately, so I called her apartment and talked to her roommate.

Annie was a little cagey about her whereabouts, so I'm assuming she must be seeing someone."

Liv was spending a lot of time at his place these days—after all, he didn't have a roommate to make things awkward and she did. She rarely spent the night though, as he had to leave a lot earlier than she did and the bus didn't run anywhere near his place. But it wasn't *every* night. They each had lives they had to live. It *was* a lot of time, though. He'd tell her she needed to quit ignoring her brother every time he called while she was with him. "I wouldn't know."

"Well, could you somehow work it into the conversation on your way home?"

He nearly choked. "Why are you so concerned about your sister's love life? That's a little disturbing—not to mention really none of your business."

"That's what Livvy says, too." He laughed and shrugged. "I'm just curious. I want her to be happy, and I refuse to feel bad about that."

Evan liked to think that Olivia *was* happy—maybe not in the way Jory probably meant, but she certainly seemed happy enough for the time being.

And he liked to think that part of that was because of him.

It struck him that he was happy, too. More relaxed. That was definitely Olivia, he decided. It was a weird kind of thing—more than the average friends-with-benefits, but not a *relationship*—but it worked for them. And he was having a very good time. "I'm sure she's fine, Jory. Leave her alone and let her live her life. You two have always been pretty tight. She'll let you know if she needs you."

"I can hope." Jory went to get another round from the fridge, and by the time he got back he'd moved on to other topics, thank heavens. The weird uncomfortable feeling that settled on his shoulders from talking about Olivia lifted and everything felt normal again.

But when he finally stumbled into bed, bleary-eyed from drinking half the night with Jory, he realized he was missing her.

And frankly, drunk or not, that scared him a little.

Olivia was all smiles and teary hugs goodbye when he picked her up Friday afternoon, but the smiles faded as soon as they turned the corner and she collapsed back against the seat and rubbed her temples. "I love them so much and miss them tons, but *whoa*...I knew there was a reason I moved to Miami and not Tampa."

He laughed. "Beyond the fact Miami offered you a contract?"

She shot him a level look. "You're assuming Ballet Tampa never offered."

"So they did?"

"Of course they did. I just didn't want to go back to Tampa. I've had offers from lots of different companies over the years, and I've been fortunate enough to be able to be picky. I already told you I had a list of places I wanted to dance—both foreign and domestic—and as long as those offers were coming in, I wasn't about to move home." She pointed a finger at him and warned, "But don't tell my folks that or I'll have to kill you."

"I've got no room to talk, so we're good."

"I want to see them and spend time with them, but I can only handle short periods of it before I feel smothered. I know the smothering comes from me being gone, but because I've been gone so long, I'm not used to being smothered. Does that make sense?"

"Yep."

"Good, because I'm not sure I fully understand it."

"You've lived away from home for a long time and you're very independent. It doesn't mean they're not great people or that you don't love them."

"They are, and I do." She sighed. "Ugh. I'm a terrible child."

"No, you're not. You're living your life—which is exactly what you should do. *And* exactly what Dee and Gary *want* you to do. They're so unbelievably proud of you."

"Thank you for that. I feel a little better." She reached over and squeezed his hand. He returned the squeeze. Then Olivia pulled out her seemingly bottomless bag of pointe shoes and ribbons and threaded a needle.

"You just sewed a bunch of shoes the other day. How many pairs of those things do you need?"

"More than you might think." She was quick and efficient, finishing with one ribbon by biting off the thread. Then she tied a new knot and started on another ribbon. "Did you and Jory have a good time?"

"Yep. And I'm supposed to ask you if you're see-ing someone."

"*Ouch.*" Olivia pulled the needle out of her thumb and sucked on the wound to soothe it. "Are you kid-ding me? Why would he care?"

"Hey, your mom asked me the same thing. You know, you could really save me some awkward mo-ments by returning their calls."

"I *do*. Eventually. I've just been a bit busy recently and there are only so many hours in a day. Given the choice between being with you and calling my fam-ily…" She shot him a sly smile. "I chose you."

"I'm flattered." And he was. More than he really should be. More than he was comfortable with, actu-ally, for a multitude of reasons.

But it was still kind of nice.

And that was also was also a little scary.

Thanksgiving pretty much marked the end of any kind of normality in Olivia's life—until at least after Christ-mas. She was prepared, though. She'd done her Christ-mas shopping in October and had had her Christmas cards addressed and ready to go since Halloween. She was used to the craziness of December—the run outs to various schools, the photo calls, music rehearsals, tech rehearsals, dress rehearsals, appearances on morn-ing shows, the evening news and at half a dozen area events. That was on top of the usual classes, doctors' appointments and the like. Oh, and the sixteen or so ac-tual performances they'd do over the next three weeks, of course. It was nonstop between now and Christmas Eve, but once the curtain closed that night, she could retreat to her bed and not be required to surface again until after the New Year.

It was the nature of the business—especially now that she was a principal—and while the schedule was grueling at times, she loved it.

But she'd never tried to do it before while she was seeing someone—or at least someone who wasn't also doing *The Nutcracker* and keeping a schedule equally as insane as hers. And *that* was a problem.

Evan, bless him, said he understood, but anyone would get frustrated when they were being shoehorned into a schedule—meals had to be grabbed during holes in that schedule, but they weren't exactly leisurely affairs at nice restaurants. Late nights with endless hours of athletic, sweaty sex were out of the question, too. She needed sleep—lots of it. She wasn't complaining—much—as it was still *good* sex, but it was rather like being put on a restricted diet after unlimited trips to the dessert bar.

After a week of rushed encounters and last-minute cancellations, Olivia was sure Evan would be over it. Surprisingly though, he wasn't. She had to give him credit for that.

The real problem, though, was that she was worried about it at all. She'd had more than one guy hit the road when faced with the truth of her priorities—and where they ranked on that list. It hadn't bothered her before.

So while it was sweet that Evan was trying to handle it, the scary part was that she was juggling, trying to create time just for him. It created stress she didn't need, but she couldn't not see him, either.

She had most of today and all of tonight off to rest up before tomorrow's opening. She could make it up to him—at least a little.

Funny, since when did she care?

She left class, ran her errands and went home. After a fast shower, she pulled a T-shirt on and crawled under the covers for a quick nap before Evan got off work.

"Olivia. Liv. *Olivia*."

She fought her way back to consciousness. Evan sat on the edge of her bed, shaking her gently. Groggy and disoriented, she squinted at him. "What are you doing here?"

"Annie let me in. When you didn't show for dinner or answer your phone, I thought something bad had happened to you."

Details came into focus. Her room, which had been flooded with daylight when she lay down, was now dim and shadowy. A glance at the clock told her she was supposed to meet Evan over an hour ago.

"Sorry. I was up at four-thirty this morning to do *Wake Up, Miami!*. I only meant to lay down for an hour or so." She reached for the bottle of water beside her bed—gone warm a long time ago—and drank deeply to wake herself the rest of the way up. "Let me change and we'll go."

"Are you actually hungry?"

"Not really," she answered honestly. "But you probably are."

He shook his head. "Why don't you go back to sleep, then. You look tired. I'll talk to you later." There was a strange, almost annoyed, undertone to his voice.

"I said I was sorry."

"I know."

"This is a really busy time for me. I warned you," she reminded him.

"I know."

"Then why are you mad?"

"I'm not," he insisted.

"You seem like it."

"Olivia, what do you want me to say? No, I'm not loving the situation, but—"

"It's only going to get worse once we open."

"And I said I understand. I can live with it, even if neither of us likes it very much."

And this was where the problems began. She sat up and faced him. "That's the thing, Evan. I *do* like this. I *love* it. I got my dream job, and I don't regret anything I gave up to get here or begrudge anything I have to do to stay here. And I can't have a boyfriend who can't accept that this is who I am and what I do."

Evan looked shocked. "I didn't realize that's where we were."

The comment didn't make sense, and the way Evan was avoiding eye contact and looking distinctly uncomfortable had her mentally replaying what she'd said. "Sorry, I didn't mean *boyfriend* boyfriend. It's just easier and quicker to say that than 'the guy I'm sleeping with'."

"Oh. Okay then."

Was that disappointment in his voice? The moment got really heavy and awkward and tense. She swallowed, sucking up her courage to go out on that limb. "I like you, Evan. I always have—except when I didn't," she corrected. "And I like *this*. What we have and what we're doing. But I'm not in a huge rush for it to be more, and I certainly don't need it to be less."

"I like this, too." He smiled, and it was possibly the sweetest, most vulnerable smile she'd ever seen on his face. She felt her heartstrings twang. "And I like you, too."

This was now officially a *moment*—bed head and all. But should she address it? Was it something she really wanted to explore right now? She didn't even fully understand what she was doing and deep contemplation—much less talking about it—might just screw it up.

She took the easier path. "Sorry I stood you up." She ran a hand down his arm. "But I do feel much better after my nap."

"You do, hmm?" Evan crawled onto the bed on all fours. Once in front of her, he sat back on his haunches and brushed her hair off her face, tucking it behind her ears. Then, holding her chin, he leaned in for a kiss. It was sweet, gentle even, with a new wealth of meaning behind it that caused her heartstrings to twang again.

She deepened the kiss, hooking her fingers in his

belt loops to hold him in place, and Evan's hands eased gently over her shoulders and down her back to gather her shirt in his hands and pull it up and off, leaving her completely naked.

Evan, though, didn't seem to be in any rush. He laid her back, watching her with hooded eyes as his fingers tickled over her skin—cheekbone to collarbone, sternum to navel and hip to hip before reversing course and ending up at her lips. It definitely had the desired effect—revving her engines and causing her breath to shallow. But there was something else, too; something new and unusual and unexpected going on inside her. She didn't want to examine it too closely, but it gave everything an additional buzz.

With Evan taking his sweet time covering nearly every inch of her in hot kisses, that buzz amplified to all-out tremors, leaving her a quivering mess barely able to return his kiss when he finally returned to her lips. In the process, he'd shucked his clothes without her noticing, and skin slid over skin in a hot caress. She reached for him, only for him to move her hands over her head and press them into the pillow. "I got this," he whispered.

That promise was nearly enough to push her over the edge without any additional assistance, but Evan was far from done. It was slow, delicious torture that left her biting her fist and gasping for air as the shock waves rocked her.

When he finally knelt between her thighs, sliding inside her with one smooth thrust, she came hard and fast. Evan didn't let it break, pounding into her, keeping her orgasm rolling longer than she dreamed possible, the intensity nearly causing her to black out.

It took forever for her breath to slow and for her vision to clear, but the sound of Evan's heart beating nearly out of his chest told her she hadn't gone there alone.

Good.

This was new, different and kind of scary. But it wasn't *bad* either, so she wasn't sure what to do...

When Evan pulled the covers up over them both, she figured she'd rest for a little while, then they'd go down to the diner for a late—make that very late, she corrected herself after glancing at the clock—dinner.

She slept straight through 'til morning and woke up alone.

There was a note propped against the clock, though.

*When you've got time, I've got time. Have a great show. *E*

That afternoon when she went back to her dressing room after warm-up class, she found a huge bouquet of flowers that brightened the room and filled it with the most wonderful smell.

The card read, *And you've got this. Be amazing to-night.*

For someone who said he made a terrible boyfriend, Evan wasn't doing too badly at all.

That freaked her out a little.

The fact she was liking it, though?

That freaked her out a lot.

* * *

Evan didn't expect security to stop him at the stage door. In retrospect, it made sense, but who would have thought backstage crashers would be such a problem at the ballet? The security guard called down to Olivia's dressing room for permission, made him sign in and then *finally* gave him directions down a labyrinth of hallways to a door with Olivia's name and picture on it. She called "Come in," seconds after his knock. "That was fast."

"I brought you your lunch…" He trailed off. Olivia was in sweats, barefaced and reclining on a leather doctor's-office-style couch, one foot submerged in a bucket on the floor, steam rising off the water. "What happened?"

She shrugged. "Stupid new shoes rubbed a blister. I'll be fine by showtime. The hot salty water helps."

Hot salty water on an open wound? "You're insane."

Keeping her foot in the bucket, she sat up. "Actually, I'm *starving.*" She held out her hands for the bag he was carrying. "Please and thank you."

There was another rather ratty-looking chair, and he sat as Olivia tore into the bag. Looking around, he said, "This is not at all what I pictured your dressing room would look like." It was a small room, with the couch and chair on one side, and a table with a mirror surrounded by lights attached to the far wall. A metal bar hanging from the ceiling held an assortment of colorful costumes. The table was cluttered with makeup and the flowers he'd sent last night. But the cinder block

walls and painted concrete floor were drab and gray
and depressing and he told her so.

"Hey, this is like the Ritz compared to what the
corps is in downstairs. At least I have some privacy.
And my own bathroom."

"How was the matinee?"

"Good," she answered around a mouthful of hummus and veggies.

"Even with the blister?"

"I've had worse. So what have you been up to?
You're kind of dressed up for a Saturday."

He leaned back and watched her carefully. "I went
to the ballet."

Olivia paused mid-chew to look at him. When he
nodded, she swallowed. "Seriously?"

"Yep."

"You were in the audience? For the matinee?"

"Yeah. You were great, by the way. I couldn't tell
anything was wrong with your foot at all."

She looked pleased. "Wow. I thought you didn't like
the ballet."

"I like *you*," he clarified. "The jury's still out on the
whole ballet thing."

"See, it wasn't as awful and boring as you expected."

"It had a few moments there that were a little tough,
but overall, no. And you're just amazing to watch."

Her cheeks turned slightly pink. "I'm impressed.
And very flattered you came."

"I thought you were starving."

"That, too." She started to take another bite, but

stopped. "Is that why you were able to get here so quickly?"

"Yeah. I was going to come backstage and surprise you, but you texted me first. By the way, I had no idea the TSA guarded your doors."

"There are some people who like the ballet a little too much, but mostly security's there to keep random people from wandering in just to see what's going on."

She popped the last bite of her sandwich into her mouth and sighed contentedly. "That was perfect and much appreciated. I'll save the fruit for later. Can you hand me that towel?"

Once she'd dried her foot off, she crossed behind him to the door. The click of the lock got his attention and, a second later, Olivia was climbing into his lap, her thighs straddling his.

"Don't you need to conserve your energy for tonight's show?" He asked the question seriously, but his hands were already cupping under her butt to pull her closer. This wasn't what he'd come for, but watching Olivia dance still had a powerful effect on his libido.

"I think I've got *just* enough energy for a quickie *and* tonight's show." She started unbuttoning his shirt as she spoke.

"Good, because I expect my money's worth out of my ticket tonight. It's supposedly a very good seat."

Her fingers paused. "You're coming again tonight?"

"Yep. I wanted to see you do all your parts."

She leaned forward to kiss his neck.

"Is this because I brought you food or because I watched a ballet?"

She grinned. "Both." Her fingers quickly finished with the last few buttons. She pushed his shirt open and ran her hands over his chest. Then she caught his eye. "And, more importantly, it's *neither*."

CHAPTER EIGHT

OLIVIA HAD CHANGED out of her tutu into a robe and was removing her makeup when the security guard at the stage door called down to get approval for her parents to come backstage. A few minutes later, there was a knock at her door.

Mom was misty-eyed as she wrapped her in a big hug. "You were wonderful, baby."

"Thanks, Mom."

Daddy handed her a bouquet of roses, his big smile saying all that and more as he hugged her. Jory hugged her, too, then made a crack about how sweaty she was. "But you just get better each time I see you. Great show."

"I'm so glad y'all could come." That was true. Knowing that family or friends were in the audience gave her a little extra boost and a real reason to smile.

"They told everyone in the surrounding two rows how talented and amazing you are and how very proud they are of you," Jory said. "It was all I could do to hush them when the Overture started."

"Because it's true," Mom insisted, completely unashamed of her behavior.

"Yes," Jory agreed, "but if you keep annoying people around us, they're going to make us start sitting in the top of the balcony."

"Why don't you go change?" Daddy said. "I'm sure you're hungry." Ever since her very first show, her parents always took her out afterward for pancakes. She was too far away for many years for it to happen as often as she liked, but it was something she was definitely looking forward to doing more often now. The family made themselves comfortable as she grabbed her clothes and took them to the bathroom to get dressed.

When she came out a few minutes later, her mom was hanging up her costumes neatly and tidying her makeup table. "You don't have to do that, Mom."

"Old stage mom habits die hard. But now that you're out, I'll get some water for the flowers."

The theater provided a couple of vases just for this reason, and Mom arranged the roses they'd brought as Olivia took her hair down and brushed it out the best she could. Jory and Daddy were flipping through their programs.

"So many pretty flowers," Mom said.

The bouquet she'd received onstage tonight sat in water on the small table in front of Daddy and Jory, ready to be reused tomorrow. A smaller bouquet of violets and daisies from Theo sat on the shelf above her mirror next to the bouquet Evan sent on opening night—which was now looking a little worse for wear, but still pretty. The flowers Evan sent last night were on her makeup table, taking up too much room, but she liked them there.

Mom set the new flowers next to Theo's bouquet. "So who's this 'E' that's sending you flowers?" she asked.

Olivia sent up a silent thanks that Evan signed the cards in the flowers with just the one initial. And while the handwriting was masculine, she assumed Mom wouldn't recognize Evan's handwriting... *Crap, but Jory would easily.* She should have pulled the cards out and hid them away.

She kicked her "getting ready" mode into high gear before Daddy or Jory decided to join this conversation. "Just a friend."

"A *special* friend from the looks of those flowers." Mom smiled as she said it.

"A supportive friend," she corrected. She tied her shoes and stood. "I'm starved. Who's ready for IHOP?"

"Are you sure you wouldn't rather go someplace nicer?" Mom asked. "Evan sent us a list of restaurants that were open late."

Daddy shook his head. "We can't break tradition. Dancers are a superstitious lot."

"Exactly, Daddy. Dinner anywhere else could jinx the whole run of shows."

"Well, I guess we can't have that."

Most of the conversation in the car and after they arrived at the restaurant revolved around the show—the differences between this choreography and the choreography in other productions she'd danced. Her family weren't necessarily experts, but they certainly had a higher than average knowledge of repertoire, thanks to her.

Over pancakes, Jory changed the subject. "We were looking through the program during intermission and some of the dancers have a 'Sponsored by Such-and-Such Company' under their bios. What's that about?"

Just a reminder that she still didn't have one. "It's just another way for the company to raise money." She explained the program briefly, while downplaying its importance and her own need.

"Well, if you need a sponsor, honey," her dad said, "The Bay Café would be proud to. No one needs to know it's your family."

Since that was exactly what she *didn't* want, she was glad that lie she'd told Annie was easily available and believable. "Thanks, Daddy, but the sponsors need to be local. I'm still new in town and people don't know me yet. But after *Nutcracker* is over, folks will know who I am. I'm sure I'll get one in the New Year." *Fingers crossed.*

"So are you thinking you'll stay here for a while then?" he asked.

"That's my plan. I love Miami, it's close to y'all, and MMBC is great. I've decided if they offer me a multiyear contract, I'll take it."

Jory laughed. "*You?* Commit to a multiyear contract? My world is askew at the thought."

She punched him in the arm. "I've even been looking at getting my own place—an actual home where I can have my stuff and grow flowers and things. And when I retire, Miami will be a good place to launch my next career."

"We really didn't realize that when we sent you off at fifteen that it would take you twelve years to find your way back. Not that we're not proud of everything you've accomplished," Mom added quickly, "but it's nice to hear you're wanting to settle down close to home."

"What about your itchy feet?" Jory asked.

She shrugged. "There will always be guest artist appearances or touring troupes, so if my feet get *too* itchy, I can do that. If not, I'm still good. I've checked off most of the dream cities on my list, and that's more than most people can say."

"Most people aren't as good as you."

"Thanks, Daddy. But this decision means that maybe next year when you come and see me dance you won't have to stay in a hotel."

"But it's a tradition," Mom protested, "and you don't need company in your house when you need your rest more. And," she said, looking at her watch, "that's probably our cue to take you home so you can get a good night's sleep. Is it just a matinee or do you have an evening show too, tomorrow?"

"Just the matinee."

"We'd love to see it, sweetheart, but we've got a big party to cater tomorrow evening and need to get on the road early."

"It's that time of year. Busy for everyone. I'm just glad you could come." She meant that.

"I'm staying at Evan's tonight and heading for a meeting in Key West tomorrow," Jory said. "Can I grab you for brunch or a cup of coffee?"

"Maybe. I've got an eleven-thirty call time, so it really depends on how early you get up."

Jory dropped their parents back at their hotel, then took Olivia home on his way to Evan's—which she'd carefully purged yesterday of any of her personal items left there. She didn't like the stealth and deception, but Evan was adamant about it.

It felt juvenile and it annoyed her, but right now was not the time to make that stand. She had enough on her plate at the moment, and there wasn't a rush. She was having a good time with Evan, but for how long? Why stir up a mess if this was just going to spin itself out? If it turned into something else, something stronger, then they'd *have* to address it, and she'd deal with that when the time came.

She waved Jory off, not expecting to see him in the morning. Knowing him and Evan both, there'd be much drinking tonight and hellacious hangovers in the morning—at least for Jory.

Sure enough, a text pinged into her phone as she was getting up the next morning. The lack of capitalization, punctuation and basic grammar skills spoke clearly to the pain of Jory's hangover and his need for more sleep. She laughed, then texted him three more times, twenty minutes apart, just to bug him.

That's what siblings were for, after all.

Evan texted her a couple of hours later, offering to pick her up after the show, which told her Jory had finally gotten up and on the road. It was a nice, bright, sunshiny day, so Jory had to be hurting for his drive down to the Keys. Evan, though, claimed to be fine.

It still sat wrong on her—basically *your brother's gone now, so we can have sex again.* But she told herself there'd be plenty of time to dive into that later on.

After all, this was the biggest, most exciting time of the year for her, job-wise, *and* she had a pseudoboyfriend on the side. Her life didn't suck, that was for sure.

So she should just enjoy it.

Evan left work early on Monday, eager to get home. He'd left Olivia asleep in his bed when he left this morning—which was a new and unusual experience for him—and, according to her, she was going to be lazy all day and he just might still find her there when he got home.

He wouldn't mind that at all, he thought with a grin.

But he had no such luck. Instead, Olivia was on his living room floor, one leg pulled up over her head in a stretch that made his hamstring hurt just looking at it. But, *damn*, she was flexible, and that, as always, stirred up his blood.

She didn't acknowledge his arrival, but then he saw the wires running from the iPod strapped to her arm to her ears. She had a light sheen of sweat on her forehead and chest, and her cheeks were flushed. When he squatted down next to her and nudged her, Olivia jumped—nearly kicking him in the face as she did.

"Sorry," she said, pulling the buds out of her ears. "Didn't hear you."

"I thought you were just going to have an easy day and relax."

"I am." She lay back down and pulled her other knee to her chest, unfolding her leg until her toes touched the ground behind her shoulder.

"And you consider this relaxing?"

"Just some Pilates and stretches so I don't get all stiff. Plus, I can only nap and read for so long before I get bored." She peeked at him around her ankle. "I was planning to shower and get dressed before you got home, but you're earlier than I thought you'd be."

He couldn't help himself. He ran a hand over the thigh displayed so beautifully in front of him. "I gotta say, this is a nice view to come home to, though."

She grinned, releasing her leg and hooking it around his shoulder to pull him closer for a kiss. "You're so easy to please."

He kissed her long and slow, loving the way she wrapped herself around him like a vine. It was a nice thing to come home to. Actually, *she* was nice to come home to. Nice and not at all as awful as he'd always thought it would be. It was something he could get used to. The realization pulled him up short.

Olivia untangled herself with a sigh and a moan. "I'm going to go get cleaned up and changed. I'm hungry."

"For someone so skinny, you eat a lot."

"That's because you keep helping me burn off all the calories. It's excellent cardio." With a wink and a sexy smile, she disappeared into his room. He heard the water running a second later.

There were various bits and pieces of exercise equipment and dance gear lying around, his fridge was full of healthy snacks and the whole place smelled vaguely of Olivia. He liked that, too. Especially how that scent clung to his sheets—and sometimes his clothes—giving him a whiff of her even when she wasn't around.

And he wanted her around more often.

He was man enough and honest enough to admit he was in strange, uncharted waters, but he had no regrets. Things had moved quickly—almost disturbingly so—but it wasn't as if they'd started off five weeks ago as strangers.

Ending things with Olivia nine years ago had been the right thing—he still stood by the intention if not the execution—but neither of them had been in the right place anyway. Now maybe they were. It was worth a shot, right?

As if he'd just tempted the Fates, his phone rang—Jory's ringtone, reminding him of a possible problem ahead, but one he was willing to tackle this time.

Just not at this moment. Not yet.

He took the phone to the patio to answer.

"Hey. How's the head?"

"I don't know what the hell you put in my drink, but

I'm just now feeling human again. I had to go to dinner last night feeling like death warmed over."

"The tequila was your idea."

"Sometimes when I'm around you I seem to forget we're nearly thirty, and I can't drink like that anymore."

"Just keeping you young at heart, my friend."

Jory made a sound suspiciously like a snort. "Anyway…I've got a big favor to ask."

"What kind of favor?"

"It's about Olivia."

Carefully, as if Jory would somehow be able to tell that Liv was currently in his shower simply by the tone of his voice, he said, "Okay."

"She was telling us the other night about some kind of sponsorship thing the company does. Businesses or individuals give money to sponsor a particular dancer and in return, get all kinds of perks the regular donors don't get. Looking at the program I got the other night, Olivia's the only dancer—outside the corps— who doesn't have one of those sponsors. She tried to downplay it, but I think it's something she needs—especially if she's going to get to stay in Miami."

Something crawled over his skin and warning bells went off in his head.

"Dad offered, of course," Jory continued, "but Livvy said it needed to be local businesses."

"How much?"

"I'm not sure exactly and the website doesn't say, but based on what I've been able to research online, several thousand dollars, at least."

"I see. And you're asking me to sponsor her."

"If not you, maybe you know someone who could? She's still new in Miami and doesn't know a lot of people with that kind of money."

But she knew me. "I'll see what I can do." It was all he could manage to say right now.

"I know it's awkward, but…"

"Not at all," he lied.

"Thanks. I'll see you next week when I'm headed back through."

"Yep. Have fun down there."

This was what it felt like to have a bubble burst. He didn't want to believe the dark thoughts creeping in, but they had merit and couldn't be dismissed out of hand. If Olivia needed this sponsorship, why hadn't she mentioned it? The fact she hadn't mentioned it at all—directly or indirectly—seemed glaringly, suspiciously *off*.

All those happy thoughts from earlier slammed into this new information, making him wonder if he'd been a fool.

A few minutes later, Olivia joined him on the patio. She was casually dressed, hair braided back off her face, minimal makeup. She took the other chair and propped her feet—in socks of course—up on a planter. "It's nice out here."

"Yeah."

She looked at him funny, but kept her voice light as she tried again. "We should eat outside tonight. Maybe grill something."

"If you want."

"You could even have a nice steak. Give the chicken a break for the evening." She laughed, then got quiet when he didn't join her. "What's wrong?"

He had neighbors, so he wasn't going to have this conversation outside. "You want a beer?"

"Sure." She followed him inside, leaning against the counter as he opened the beers and handed her one.

"I was just thinking," he started in a conversational tone, "You never did tell me why you got in touch after all these years."

For a brief second—literally a flash he would have missed if he hadn't been watching her so closely—Olivia looked uncomfortable. *Yeah, there was something she was hiding.*

Just as quickly, she was shrugging as if it was nothing. "It seemed weird to be in the same town and not get in touch. And I thought it might make things easier for Jory in the long run if we had a truce in place. And I'm glad I did. Think how awkward Thanksgiving *could* have been otherwise."

"For Jory. Who we're not telling about us."

An eyebrow went up. "That was more your idea, not mine."

But she hadn't fought too hard about it either. He let that pass for the time being, wanting to get his biggest suspicions confirmed or denied. "But why? It's not like we parted on good terms."

"I guess I decided to get over it and let go of a ridiculous grudge."

"Jory says you never let go of a grudge."

"Jory's not the expert on me he seems to think he is." She placed her beer carefully on the counter and met his eyes. "What is this all *really* about?"

Well, he wasn't getting anywhere the indirect way. "I understand you need some kind of sponsorship."

She blinked in surprise. "How do you know about that?"

"Because Jory just called me and asked if I'd do it."

"Darn. I'm sorry. He shouldn't have done that." She shook her head and reached over to touch his hand. "I told him not to worry about it, but I should have known he'd call you."

"Of course he did. He says you need a local sponsor and hey, I'm local."

"I only said that so that my folks—and Jory for that matter—wouldn't try to do it."

"But you do need the sponsorship."

"I don't *need* it," she corrected, withdrawing her hand. "It would be nice to have it, but—"

"And just like Jory, I was the one person in Miami who you knew would have the money. Was that why you contacted me wanting to get together?"

He could almost see the wheels turning in her head as she decided how to answer. Finally, she took a deep breath and exhaled slowly. "Yes, but—"

That hurt worse than expected. "I'd have given it to you, Olivia. All you had to do was ask. You didn't have to sleep with me first."

"*Whoa.* Don't even go there. One has nothing to do with the other." He could tell he'd offended her, but that didn't give him any truths. "I'd gotten myself into a panic thinking I *had* to get that sponsorship if I wanted a contract for next season, and yes, I figured you would be the obvious choice."

"Because of my friendship with Jory? Or because you felt I owed you after what happened with us?"

She didn't address that statement, making him assume he'd scored there, too. "It was a bad plan. I admit that now. I decided—at dinner, after I actually saw you again and talked to you—that it would be tacky to even ask because there was too much other stuff between us. And you made it very clear you had no interest in donating. I let it go and I was okay with that."

"So leaving your phone in my car was just a happy accident?"

"Of course it was." Her eyebrows pulled together. "How conniving do you think I am?"

"Honestly, Olivia, I don't know anymore. I was led blindly into this."

"Oh, *please*. You all but made a pass at me at Tourmaine's. You flat-out propositioned me the very next night. It was clear what you wanted."

"What was I supposed to think? You called me out of the blue. I thought that was what *you* wanted."

"So your feelings are hurt because you feel misled? Or is it because I hadn't been pining over you all these years?" She turned to look at him evenly, and some of the snark and the heat left her voice. "What difference does it make why I called you *then?* It has nothing to do with where we are now."

"It doesn't?"

She pulled back as though he'd slapped her. "Excuse me?"

"Surely you were planning to ask me for it eventually."

Olivia's jaw tightened. "If you don't quit implying that I'm some kind of prostitute, I'm going to kick your butt so hard you'll be coughing up ribbons from my pointe shoes tomorrow."

He'd definitely hit a nerve. "I don't know why you're so surprised I'd think that."

"Maybe because we've spent a lot of time together and you should know me better than that. Or at least be willing to give me the benefit of the doubt."

"My apologies. I'm a little thrown by this. I mean, at least I came into this honestly, with the mistaken assumption you were, too. You know, like mature adults."

Her jaw dropped. "Oh no, don't you dare start tossing out words like 'honesty' and 'maturity' like you have a clue what either one of them means. *I'm* not the one who's lying to my supposed best friend because I don't want anyone to know that we're sleeping together."

"That's different."

"How?" she snapped. "Either you're an adult or you're not."

"You're changing the subject."

"Not really. I may have come into this a little dishonestly, but you're still wallowing in the lies. And you're making me your accomplice when I have nothing to hide." Her eyes narrowed as she crossed her arms over her chest. "Or am I just a convenient bed buddy with an expiration date looming, and *that's* why you don't want to tell Jory?"

"You're not exactly pushing hard to tell him either. I could assume you don't want him to know his sweet baby sister is sleeping with his best friend again when it'll all be over once you get your money."

She slapped him. Hard. The crack echoed in the room. "I'm *not* sleeping with you for money. Right now, I'm not sure why I'm seeing you at all." She stormed out of the room.

There'd been a delay between the sound of the slap and the sensation, but as blood rushed to his cheek, it began to sting. He rubbed it gently. He couldn't get too angry about it, though; she *had* warned him.

He wasn't sure who was in the right and who was in the wrong, but it wasn't pretty either way.

He could hear Olivia talking, but to whom was the question. As he came out of the kitchen, Olivia nearly ran him down in the hallway. She had her phone to her ear and her bags draped over her shoulder. "Thank you," she said and hung up, shoving the phone into her pocket.

Dodging around him without a word, she gathered up her stuff out of the living room.

"You're leaving?"

"Yep," she snapped.

"How? You don't have a car."

"I've got a cab on the way." She didn't have that much stuff, and it didn't take her long to load it up.

"Olivia…"

She spun on him, her eyes hot with anger. "I'm not going to stay here and let you continue to cast aspersions on my character just for the opportunity to be another notch in your bedpost. Not again. It's not worth it." She paused at the door. "And just to be clear… I don't need your money. I'm very good at what I do and *that's* what matters most. But even if I had to choose, I'd rather go home and teach preschoolers at the local Toe, Tap and Twirl than take a dime of sponsorship money from you. Goodbye, Evan." She slammed the door hard enough to shake the frame.

Well, that wasn't what he'd planned for this evening, and it was a big turn from where he'd started just an hour ago.

But what else could he have expected?

CHAPTER NINE

RAGE AND INSULT propelled Olivia into the parking lot of Evan's condo, where she paced while waiting for her taxi to arrive. Her eyes burned, but the anger was too strong to let the tears fall.

The fact there were tears at all shocked her. There was so much to be angry about, but tears meant something else. Tears meant she was hurt, and she didn't want to be hurt. She shouldn't even be in a place where Evan *could* hurt her. But those tears threatening to fall meant she was in that place—even if this was the first time she'd realized it—and that knowledge only made everything worse.

But maybe it was better to know now, before she got in any deeper. Evan hadn't changed all that much after all—*the selfish, egotistical jerk*. She'd at least admitted where she was wrong; Evan couldn't even see that he might be, much less admit it.

Maybe Jory had been right all along, trying to keep her and Evan apart. She'd been too caught up in her own infatuation and hormones to realize that Jory might have sound reasons. Maybe Evan knew those reasons were sound as well and *that's* why he'd been so adamant about keeping Jory in the dark. Jory might have told her more than Evan wanted her to know.

Not everything you wanted could be good for you, and sometimes you needed someone else to smack your hand away from the cookie jar.

In a fair and just world, men like Evan would come with warning labels tattooed on their washboard abs. She sighed. There was no reason to think she'd have paid any attention to a written warning when she'd done such a good job ignoring the real-life examples and lessons she had. Man, she was stupid.

She'd walked right into this, honestly believing it would somehow be different just because she wanted it to be. She could pass some of the blame to Evan, but she was equally as responsible for her own hurt.

Maybe a little more so, since he'd even tried to warn her.

The cabbie asked if she was okay, and after a couple of assurances on her part, he finally seemed to accept it and remained silent as he took her home. She tipped him extra, though, for his concern.

It wasn't that late, but the living room was dark and quiet as Olivia locked the door behind her. *Good.* She sighed in relief and went to the fridge for something to drink. She really tried to limit her alcohol during performance weeks, but the wine beckoned and she gave in. Taking a big swallow, she headed down the hall toward her room.

"Olivia?"

She jumped at the voice, nearly dropping her glass. "Annie! I didn't know you were here. Did I wake you?"

"No, I was just…" She changed tacks abruptly. "I thought you were staying at Evan's tonight."

"Not anymore."

Surprised turned instantly to concern. "Is everything okay?"

"Between me and Evan? No. That's pretty much over."

"Oh, Olivia, I'm sorry."

"Thanks, but I'm okay."

Annie put a hand on her arm. "Do you want to talk about it?"

Did she? Just for the sympathy even though justice was out of the question? "Thanks, I—"

"Annie?" That was a male voice. Olivia looked at Annie, who gave her a slightly embarrassed smile and shrugged. The man the voice belonged to stepped into the hallway a second later. He was shirtless and barefoot and oh-*my*-pretty to boot. Belatedly, Olivia noticed that Annie was slightly disheveled herself. "Is everything okay?" he asked.

"Stephen, this is my roommate, Olivia. Olivia, this is Stephen. We met through work."

"It's nice to meet you," she said lamely.

"And you," Stephen said. "I took my mother to see *The Nutcracker* last week. You were very good."

"Thank you." She wasn't as completely stupid as she thought, because she could still tell when she was a fifth wheel. "Please don't think I'm rude not to hang out and chat, but I'm going to go to my room now and listen to some music. Very loud music. I'll use headphones so it won't bother you."

"Good night, then," Stephen said, reaching for Annie's hand.

"Are you sure?" Annie asked. "If you need to talk, I can…"

"No," she insisted. "I'm thinking a long hot bath and an early bedtime is the probably best thing for me right now. Good night."

Headphones on and music cranked up, Olivia turned the water on and left the tub to fill. In a way, it was good that she and Annie not talk it to death and obsess over Evan or what he did or did not do. It was what it was. Wallowing wasn't good for anyone, now was as good a time as any to let it go. It had been only a little more than a month, so it wasn't as if she was deeply invested or anything.

So why the hell was she crying?

Although Evan didn't like himself much for thinking it, Jory was really the last person he wanted to see at the moment. He already felt bad enough for sleeping with Olivia and lying to Jory about it—which made it a little hard to face him—but now he had the added guilt of wanting to avoid his best friend. It was a big spiral of guilt, and he didn't like feeling guilty about anything.

And Jory made him think about Olivia—they had the same hair color, same features, same mannerisms—

when he was quite determined *not* to think about her. He felt foolish for not realizing her ulterior motives—regardless of when she abandoned those motives, and more than a little annoyed that she'd think his motives were anything more than protection for all of them.

He might be selfish occasionally, but he usually had a good reason why.

If not for Olivia, he'd be happy to have Jory here. It was just difficult to act as if everything was perfectly normal, the same as it was before Olivia decided to walk back into his life.

And while Jory had spent the week on a half business, half scuba diving trip in Key West, *he'd* spent the week working on *not* thinking about Olivia and trying to forget the past month or so. They were in vastly different moods because of this.

They'd gone easy on the booze last night as Jory was still cussing him for the hangover last Sunday, and he'd stated early on in the evening that he would *not* be doing the four-hour drive home today hungover, too.

Evan was drinking coffee and half watching the news when Jory, freshly showered, shaved and not hungover, came in carrying a cup and staring at his phone.

"Mom says to tell you she's moving Christmas dinner to the twenty-sixth this year," Jory said, reading off his phone. "Olivia has a Christmas Eve performance, and Mom doesn't want her to have to rush home on the twenty-fifth. So everything is shifting a day later."

"Actually, I don't think I'll be able to come this year."

"Why not?"

The surprise tinged with disappointment made him feel a little better. "I've had another invitation."

"From who?"

"I do have other friends, you know."

Jory sat. "You've had Christmas dinner at our house for nearly ten years. If you have other friends, they've been stingy with the invites up to now."

Olivia had always been in another city, usually unable to make it to her parents' until after he left. It had worked fine in the past, but this year...definitely not. "Maybe it's a new friend."

Jory snorted. "Because you make *those* so easily and often."

"Hmm, I'm beginning to think I might have one friend too many right now."

"Mom will be disappointed."

He'd rather have Dee disappointed than horrified. Olivia obviously hadn't said anything to her family about what happened—and he was grateful for that—but that might change if she were forced to share her holiday with him now. If he wanted to salvage what he had with the Madison family, he needed to stay away. He should have stayed away from Olivia altogether if for no other reason than respect for Jory and Gary and Dee.

But he was selfish, as usual, and arrogant, as well, thinking he could have his cake and eat it, too.

"Is it Olivia?"

Was Jory a mind reader now? "What?"

"Y'all seemed okay at Thanksgiving, but I realize now that may have been just for Mom and Dad's benefit. If that was all an act, I can understand why you wouldn't be up for another round."

"Look, I had to tell Olivia the truth about what happened. She deserved to know that it wasn't about her." He couldn't tell Jory the full truth, but he should—and could—tell him that much. There were enough secrets in this freaky triangle, and *that* one needed to be put to bed for good.

Jory coughed. "I'm surprised she didn't come after me with the carving knife."

"She wasn't happy about it, but I think I got her to see your point. You weren't wrong, and you did mean well."

"I'm sure the fact I 'meant well' went over splendidly." He rolled his eyes.

"Oh, yes, of *course* that made all the difference to her."

Jory picked up on his sarcasm. "Maybe I'll apologize then. I never really brought it up before, simply because it was easier not to."

Damn it, that wasn't what he wanted. "She's let it go. I've let it go. Why bring it up at all?"

Jory leaned back and rubbed his eyes. "You know, if you'd been *this* guy nine years ago, maybe I wouldn't have minded it so much. You and Olivia, I mean."

Evan nearly fell out of his chair, but recovered quickly. "I am the same guy."

"Nah. You're not as angry or as hell-bent on breaking every one of your parents' rules. Raising hell is fine and good—and something you needed to do for your own sake—but you were taking it to extremes. And seducing every girl that got within twenty feet of you like it was your mission in life..."

"No one wants their sister mixed up with a guy like that. I get it, Jory. No need to beat that dead horse."

"Want to hear something funny?"

"Yes, please." *Anything to change the subject.*

"About five years ago, Mom got this idea that you and Olivia would be a good match if she could ever get you two in the same room."

Evan choked.

"I know, it's crazy, huh?" Jory laughed at the thought. "She just wants you in the family, and since you're too old to formally adopt, that was her next idea. But now that Livvy is finally contemplating settling down in one place..." He let the implication hang.

Evan, though, was still sputtering and couldn't talk, which Jory seemed to read a completely different way. "Don't worry. I don't think Mom will actually push that idea, so it's safe if you change your mind and decide to come for Christmas, after all."

He coughed and cleared his throat. It was all just too much to even process.

Jory, thankfully, didn't seem to need a response. "And unless you need the Heimlich maneuver, I should probably be hitting the road."

Evan walked Jory out.

Jory tossed his overnight bag in the backseat. "Oh, by the way," he said. "I owe you an apology."

"For?"

"Dropping that sponsorship thing on you. When Olivia mentioned it, you were the first person to come to mind, and I called without thinking it through all the way."

Liv and Jory were definitely two peas in a pod. According to her, she'd done the same thing but backed out before actually making the request. "Don't worry about it."

With a nod, Jory got in his car. "And if you change your mind about Christmas, just give Mom a call and let her know. She'll make you the cookies you like."

It was barely noon and he already needed a drink. The entire Madison family seemed determined to drive him insane—but for different reasons in completely different ways.

It was insult to injury. Had he wanted Olivia partly because she was forbidden fruit? Maybe, but now that she might not be so forbidden after all, he wanted her still.

But he still couldn't have her. What had she said about men she wouldn't dance with again because they'd dropped her? Well, he'd dropped her twice. She wouldn't trust him again.

This sucked.

It also hurt more than he liked to admit, but considering the amount of hurt he'd thrown on people in the past… Well, his dear old dad would love to know Evan was reaping exactly what he'd sown, just as warned.

Call it payback, karma or divine justice—it sucked no matter what he named it.

But he'd earned it. Fairly. Olivia had every right to walk, and he couldn't fault her for doing it.

And it was probably better for her that she had.

The real question was whether he could just let her go.

Wednesday afternoon, Olivia was in the studio working on her variations for the winter special. She didn't have to be there—the rehearsal schedule was cut way back during performance weeks—but it was pretty much the only thing she knew to do with herself.

She hadn't heard from Evan in over a week. She'd rather expected—maybe *hoped* was a better word—to hear *something*, but there'd been nothing but silence. It was both good and bad.

If this really had run its course, a clean break was better in the long run—no need to draw it out. Because the past week had proven one thing to her quite clearly: although she'd let her hormones lead the way, sticking around for good sex and good times, she'd gotten in deeper than expected. Deeper than was wise.

She'd obviously learned nothing in the past nine years because she was pretty much right back where she'd been before with Evan: hurt.

Screw it. And screw him.

She'd gotten all attached to the idea of settling down

in Miami and taken it too far, insanely believing that Evan could be a part of that.

Maybe she'd been dropped on her head too many times.

It was horrifying enough to have her trolling websites from other companies, thinking a change of city might be nice.

No. She wasn't leaving Miami. Not because of him. She'd never let her emotions drive her decisions about her career, and she wasn't going to start now. Not over a guy.

She'd never had to live in the same city with an ex before—at least not for very long—but people did it all the time. It had to be possible. Miami was a big place.

Hell, as long as Jory and Evan were friends she'd never be fully away from him anyway. He'd continue to be on the fringe of her life.

She'd gotten over him before, and she'd get over him again.

She stretched and shook her legs out. *This* was what she was good at. Anger and hurt feelings could be pushed down and forgotten for a while when her feet were moving too fast for her to focus on anything else and the details required her full concentration.

This was who she was. She'd made her choice years ago.

She cued up her music.

Olivia always felt a little deflated when the curtain closed on a show for the last time—even when that show was *The Nutcracker*. Months of work and preparation—over. The adrenaline rush of performing, the energy of the audience, the lights and costumes and music—that was her drug of choice and she was a junkie.

And like a junkie who'd been riding on a major high, the crash would come. But she had a couple of hours yet to enjoy the ride. As she left the stage, Theo ran up beside her. "We have a Christmas Eve tradition here at MMBC—a greasy, high-fat, carb-loaded feast at Lucy's Diner. Do you want to come?"

"Sure." Annie had left this morning to go to her mom's in Fort Lauderdale, so she'd be going home to an empty house anyway. "When?"

"It'll take at least thirty or forty-five minutes for everyone to get packed up, but I'll come knock on your door when we're ready."

"Great." In her dressing room, she scrubbed the makeup off her face and started packing up her stuff— well, more tossing it haphazardly into a bag to be sorted later. She'd taken home all but the essentials yesterday, so there wasn't that much to pack.

Loraine, the costume mistress, came in to pick up her costumes, followed a minute later by Richard, the artistic director, who handed her a card and wished her a Merry Christmas.

"And I didn't have a chance to tell you before the show, but we got a call yesterday from a business wanting to sponsor you. That's pretty impressive for someone who's still relatively new in town."

She fought to keep her face still and her tone light. "That's wonderful. Can I ask which business?" *We've done sixteen performances, dozens of public appearances, and the* Times *did a big write-up last week. Any one of those things could have landed me a sponsor.* She realized she was holding her breath.

"The Lawford Agency. It's a newish advertising agency, but it's getting big. They haven't donated before, so extra congrats for landing us a new one."

Evan. As soon as Richard had told her she'd gotten sponsorship, she'd known it would be him. Somehow she managed to keep a smile on her face and make the proper responses, hiding the wave of mixed emotions inside her. Once Richard left though, she collapsed onto the couch and rubbed her temples.

She'd told him she didn't want his money. So why'd he do it? Was it a peace offering? Guilt money? Bribery? Payment for sexual services rendered? That one made her feel a little nauseous.

And while there was a definite feeling of relief that came with the knowledge he'd all but guaranteed that MMBC would offer her another contract, it was riding uneasily on top of the other clashing emotions.

She was still sitting there, trying to sort it out, when Theo stuck his head around the door. "You ready?"

"Yeah." She grabbed her bags and followed him out. A crowd of company members were gathered by the stage door. "Wait," she said, reaching for his elbow. "I'm going to have to pass. I just realized I have something I need to do."

Disbelieving, he blinked at her. "At eleven o'clock on Christmas Eve?"

"I know, but yes."

He gave her a careful look. "Is this something you need help or backup for? Maybe a driver for the get-away car?"

"No, but thanks." She rose up on her tiptoes and kissed his cheek. "Merry Christmas, Theo."

"Merry Christmas, Olivia."

She waved at everyone as she passed them and went to the parking deck where she'd left the car she'd rented for the drive home tomorrow. Halfway to Evan's house, she realized how very, very stupid she was being. Even if it weren't beyond rude to show up unannounced at someone's house after eleven o'clock—on *any* night, much less Christmas Eve—there was no guarantee that Evan would be home. He wasn't heading to Tampa to-morrow to be with her family, she knew that much, but that didn't mean he was staying in Miami over the holiday, either. He could be anywhere on the planet.

But she was already pulling into the parking lot, so she had nothing to lose at this point.

Evan's car was in its spot, so that improved the chances of him being home exponentially. But as she rang the doorbell, she realized that he might not be home *alone*.

Dear Lord, would she *ever* learn to not run off half-cocked on half-cooked plans? But unless she was going to ding-and-ditch, it was a little too late now.

Half an eternity passed before she finally heard

him unlocking the door. The irritated look on his face quickly turned to surprise, though, when he saw her. But he didn't say anything.

He was barefoot and wearing battered jeans and the T-shirt she sometimes wore when she was there because it was extra soft from years of washing. Although his hair was mussed and adorable, he didn't look like he'd been asleep.

At this point, she wasn't sure anymore whether she was angry or curious or what, and since she hadn't given a second's thought to what she actually wanted to say now that she was here, they ended up staring at each other in silence for a long moment.

"Olivia?"

"I told you I didn't want your money." The words just tumbled out, unplanned and very ungracefully.

"Well, it's a good thing I gave it to the Miami Modern Ballet Company and not you, then."

"You know what I mean. I never asked you to sponsor me."

"But Jory did. So I did it for him. And your parents. A small way to pay them back for all their kindness over the years."

"So it had nothing to do with me." He shrugged, and it grated over her last nerve. She hadn't wanted to cash in her family's relationship to Evan like some kind of IOU, yet she'd ended up exactly there. Hell, she should have just stuck with plan A—it would have been tacky and awkward as hell, but it would have been quicker and less painful than the long way around she took to get here. "Well." She cleared her throat, feeling like a complete fool. "Welcome to the MMBC family. Your generous donation is much appreciated, and we hope you enjoy the many benefits your sponsorship includes."

"Why are you here, Olivia?"

Such a loaded question. And one she wasn't sure she had the guts to answer. "I needed to know why you did it."

"It's only money, not arms and legs. And as you said, it's a tax deduction, and it's good PR for the agency."

A reasonable answer, even if she wasn't sure what it meant for her. Hell, she wasn't sure what answer she'd been hoping for, but that one left her feeling like a leaking balloon. "Okay, then. Sorry I bothered you. Good night and um…Merry Christmas."

She turned away before she made this any worse or more humiliating. She wouldn't run, but she could damn sure walk away quickly.

"Olivia, wait." Evan caught up with her and put a hand on her upper arm. When she turned around, he stepped back, hunching his shoulders and putting his hands in his pockets, but he didn't speak immediately. He leaned against his car. "Do you have any idea…" He stopped and thought for a second. "Your parents are better parents to me than my own. And Jory's like a brother to me."

"Yes, I know." She wouldn't mess that up for him or damage that relationship, no matter how angry or hurt she was. She was going to tell him that, but he spoke first.

"Then can you imagine how disloyal it feels to want you? Carnal exploration of their only daughter and sister seems a poor way to pay back that kindness. And wanting any more than that feels like taking too much. I'm a heartless bastard, but even I know that's a step over the line."

"I see."

"On top of that, I know that if screw things up with you, I risk losing it all. Of hurting everyone I care about in one fell swoop. It's a bad place to be in."

Lovely. She'd been doomed to this by her own loving, wonderful family. The same family she took for granted.

He sighed and stared up at the sky. "So, yeah, I tried to play both sides of the game and have it all." He shook his head and shrugged. "But I managed to screw it up anyway, which is pretty amazing even for me. I can't have you and I can't be around them without being reminded of that, so now I can't have them, either."

This was twisted, but she knew too much to not see Evan's logic. And it made her mad. "That's bull."

Another slap would have been far more preferable. In fact, *anything* would be preferable to this Greek tragedy. "No, that's the truth."

"If you won't give me any credit, at least give some to the family you claim to respect so much."

Why couldn't she see that he was just trying to do

the right thing for once? "I do respect them. And you, too, believe it or not."

"Then grow up," she snapped.

"Excuse me?"

"So your parents suck. I hate that for you, and I'm glad mine could be there for you instead. You should know them well enough to know that no matter what, they won't turn their backs on you. So drop the martyr act. Either you want me or you don't."

She made it seem so easy. "I already hurt you once. Wasn't that enough?"

"I like how you think this isn't hurting me now."

"See? You've just proven my point."

Olivia's lips thinned. Then she nodded. "Well, I guess got my answer." She turned her back on him and walked quickly toward a small black sedan.

And there it was. At least it was done and they could move on. It was for the best, really. But his feet were already moving in her direction, catching up with her before she could open the door.

When she turned around, he kissed her, fully expecting her to push him off and slap him again, so Olivia kissing him back felt like a Christmas miracle. It went on and on—desperate, but more sweet than carnal.

He steadied her as he set her on her feet and loosened his grip without letting her go. "No. *That's* your answer."

She smiled. "I like that one much better."

"Me, too, but—"

Olivia put a finger over his lips. "Let's just take this one step at a time."

"Figure out the basics, how we move together, before trying the harder stuff?" he teased.

"Exactly."

He grinned at her and got one in response. "Does that mean you're learning to trust me?"

"Maybe," she hedged.

"Then we'll have to keep working at it."

"Practice makes better."

"And I'm looking forward to it."

EPILOGUE

"It's only six weeks." She stared at the contract. She hadn't gone looking for this. She was happy in Miami. The spring show was only a couple of weeks away, and then she and Evan were going on their first official vacation as a couple. These were exciting, heady times. But now that the opportunity presented itself, her feet were itching to go.

Evan barely looked up from his tablet. "I know. You should sign the contract."

"You could come to Paris and visit me, if you wanted," she offered.

He smiled at her. "Maybe I'll do that. Sign the contract."

She refilled her wineglass, stalling for time. Things had been going so well between them the past couple of months, and she didn't want to screw it up now. Hell, she'd just moved in last week—although that had been partly precipitated by Annie wanting to move Stephen into their condo. He might think she was having second thoughts. "It's just an amazing opportunity and it fell into my lap."

"Which is exactly why you should go." He seemed calm and unbothered by the idea.

"Maybe I shouldn't. I mean, I just signed my new contract with MMBC." *Argh.* The indecision was killing her. "Maybe I should stay here and do their summer stock."

That finally got his attention. "No, you shouldn't. Sign. Go. Summer in Miami versus summer in Paris? Paris wins." He held up the pen, but she didn't take it. "Sign it. You know you want to," he said, waving the pen like a hypnotist.

"Are you trying to get rid of me?"

He rolled his eyes. "If I say yes, will you sign the contract?"

She shot him a dirty look. "Six months ago I wouldn't have thought twice about this. What is wrong with me?"

He grinned at her. "Six months ago you didn't have me."

"And *there's* the ego. I should go just because you said that."

"Exactly. *Go.*" He took her hands. "Yes, I will miss you terribly, but you should still go. I'll be here when you get back. You don't have to choose between me and your career. You can have both."

Both? She hadn't thought she'd wanted both. But now she did.

"I'll probably be ten pounds heavier because I'll

be eating whatever I want for six weeks, but I'll be here."

She leaned in to give him a kiss. "I'll still love you anyway."

Evan pulled back a little in shock. "You love me?"

Ooops. She'd been thinking it, but hadn't worked up the courage to say anything, and now.... But Evan didn't seem panicked or poised for flight, just surprised—and maybe a little pleased. That gave her courage. "Yeah. I'm pretty sure I do."

"Oh. Wow."

"Just 'wow'?" That wasn't exactly a rousing endorsement. Maybe she'd gone too far, too soon.

"I didn't know that you felt that way, I mean."

"Why would I put up with you otherwise?"

"I'm good in bed?"

She pretended to think, then shrugged. "Meh."

An eyebrow went up. "Oh, really?" Evan scooped her up and over his shoulder like a sack of potatoes, carrying her down the hall to their bedroom, where he dropped her on the bed. Climbing on top of her, he said, "That sounds like a challenge."

She was trapped between Evan and the mattress, caged by his arms—not that she was really complaining. He dropped his forehead to hers. "I love you, too."

A happy bubble filled her chest. "Wow."

"So will you go to Paris?"

She felt safe saying, "Yeah. I think so. Will you come to visit me?"

He thought for a second. "I'll come at the end to see your show. And then we'll take a week or so for vacation. How's that?"

"That sounds good." She leaned up far enough to kiss him. "*Two* vacations planned, and it's barely May. What will we plan for the fall?"

This time he didn't stop to think at all. "How about a wedding?"

She couldn't have heard that correctly. But she couldn't think of anything else that sounded like that. "A wedding?"

"Yeah. I'm thinking small and tasteful. Or big and ostentatious, it's totally up to you."

"Wow."

He looked surprised. "Just wow? That's not actually an answer, Liv."

"You haven't actually asked me a question, you know."

He grinned, and it was contagious. And while she wouldn't have thought ten minutes ago she was ready for this, she was sure it was the right decision.

"Do you trust me?"

"Yes."

"Do you love me?"

"Yes."

"Olivia Madison, will you marry me?"

"Yes, Evan, I will marry you." He kissed her then and happiness made her toes tingle. She pulled her head back and made him look at her. "One thing, though."

He pulled back, worry on his face. "What's that?"

"You get to tell Jory."

* * * * *